My LIFE of CRIME

My LIFE of CRIME

Richard W. Jennings

Houghton Mifflin Company Boston 2002

Walter Lorraine Books

Walter Lorraine (wr) Books

Copyright © 2002 by Richard W. Jennings

www.houghtonmifflinbooks.com

Library of Congress Cataloging-in-Publication Data

Jennings, Richard W. (Richard Walker), 1945–
  My life of crime / Richard W. Jennings.
    p. cm.
Summary: A sixth-grader's discovery of a bedraggled
classroom pet parrot sets him on an adventure with real
ethical and legal implications.
  ISBN 0-618-21433-X
  [1. Parrots — Fiction. 2. Stealing — Fiction. 3. Schools — Fiction.]
I. Title.
  PZ7.J4298765 My 2002
  [Fic]— dc21   2002001183

Printed in the United States of America
QUM 10 9 8 7 6 5 4 3 2 1

To Marc Jaffe

My LIFE of CRIME

Unidentified Flying Object

It all started with a feather.

It was a bright, shiny feather, a feather as long as your forefinger and as green as the equatorial rain forest. It was an unlikely, exotic sort of feather, and it was lying like a lost penny in the middle of the hall.

Naturally, I stooped over to pick it up. I had no choice. Fate had placed it there for me to find.

At the time, I was passing by the library, taking the long way around to sixth grade social studies, which, thanks to an uneventful early-morning doctor's appointment, I had nearly succeeded in missing entirely. My meandering route took me down a hallway that serves the third grade classrooms, an architectural dead end that until that moment had held absolutely no interest for me.

Third-graders! I thought. *At that age, it's not school they attend, it's daycare.*

I handed my pass to Mr. String, who waved me to my seat without bothering to read it. Only five minutes remained before the bell. I knew I should be using this time to copy the next day's assignment from the board, but the feather was too intriguing.

I opened my notebook and lay the feather gently upon a blank page. I could see that it wasn't the solid, uniform, leaf-colored green it had first appeared to be, but varied in shade from a dark olive green at the base to a glowing lime green at the tip. Most interesting of all was the presence of a small, circular, blood-red spot on one curved edge, resembling paint spatter.

Squinting, I held the feather against the bright May light streaming through the windows. The crimson dot wasn't paint, and it wasn't blood. Like the green that surrounded it, the scarlet blemish was natural pigmentation.

What kind of bird is green with red polka dots, I wondered, *and flies through the hallways of schools?*

It sounded like a riddle.

"It's probably from some third-grader's classroom project," K said when I caught up with her at lunch.

"They're always gluing common objects together and pretending that it's art."

"There's nothing common about this," I corrected her, waving the evidence in her face. "And it isn't from any little kid's crafts, because it's not painted, it's not mangled, it's not smudged with fingerprints, and it doesn't contain a single speck of glue."

K took a bite of her sandwich and frowned at me.

"I never said they were any good at what they do," she mumbled. "They probably missed a spot. Anyway, what's the big deal? It's just a feather."

It seemed foolish to argue with a person whose mouth was full of peanut butter, so I let the matter drop, even though I strongly disagreed with K.

What I held in my hand was not just a feather — I was sure of that.

It was a mystery.

Curiouser and Curiouser

My name is Fowler, which experience has made me reluctant to admit. If it were my last name, I'd have no problem with it. Unfortunately, it's my first name, and many people make fun of it.

At baseball practice, I step up to the plate when Mr. String calls out, "Batter up!"

"Foul-er up!" the kids respond, laughing as if the

tiresome joke had just occurred to them.

Oh, what I would give for an ordinary name — a name like David, or Michael, or Derek! I'd even settle for a forgettable nickname. There is no nickname for Fowler — at least, not one you'd want.

Despite this, the rest of my life is pretty ordinary. I'm average-looking, make average grades, and have parents who are so thoroughly average in every way that there's hardly anything to say about them. Both were out of town during this time. My father, an engineer, was in Asia supervising the construction of a factory to make plastic tag protectors for bean bag toys, and my mother, fond of fish, was attending cooking school in Norway. Neither was expected back any time soon. The burden of my daily welfare was mine, although K's mother had volunteered to keep an eye on me.

K lives next door. She's like a sister to me, except that whenever we begin to get on each other's nerves, one of us can always go home. It's an ideal arrangement for people who wish to remain friends.

The secret to keeping a friend is knowing when to let the other person win — the closer you can make this to always, the better.

I figured that the reason K wasn't interested in my feather was because she was jealous. Usually, she's the one who finds things. Most of the time, it's money. It's as if her feet, which are large for a girl, were metal detectors.

4

I'm still trying to figure out what I'm good at.

As soon as school was out, I met K on the sidewalk. Most days, when the weather's nice, we walk home together. This time, however, I begged off.

"I've got to check on something," I told her. "I'll catch up with you later."

"It's that feather, isn't it?" she said, picking up a quarter that lay beside the curb — some child's milk money, no doubt.

"I'm just following a hunch," I explained. "I have to pay attention to my inner voice."

"You know," she said, placing her hands on her hips and stretching her wide, expressive mouth into a clownish frown, "just because a person's inner voice is capable of speech doesn't mean it knows what it's talking about."

"I'll see you later, K," I said.

My school empties out fast in the afternoon. You'd almost think the teachers were in as big a hurry to get out of there as the kids. Vice President Lloyd, the school custodian, was running a floor buffer in the main hall. In the library, a pink-haired woman with big hips was returning books to the shelves. Otherwise, the place seemed deserted.

At the end of the cul-de-sac in which I'd found the feather were two third grade classrooms and a small office. Only the office merited a door that opened and closed. The classrooms were entered through open doorways. The building's architects must have figured that, given the chance, third-graders would accidentally lock themselves in.

One of the classrooms was silent and dark. In the other one, I could hear somebody moving around. I figured I'd better steer clear of it for the time being.

I chose wisely, because no sooner had I stepped into the darkened room than I spied two more feathers on the floor just inside the doorway, both about the same size as the one I'd found that morning. Each was green. Neither had red spots.

Hmmm, I thought. *Interesting.*

Like a searchlight, my eyes swung around to survey the room. What greeted them was the usual assortment of third grade clutter, with every wall surface papered over with simple instructions and even simpler inspirational messages:

THE SECRET TO SUCCESS IS PAYING ATTENTION!

IT COSTS YOU NOTHING TO GIVE SOMEONE YOUR SMILE!

RAISE YOUR HAND, NOT YOUR VOICE!

Yuck! I thought. *Am I glad to have this part of my life behind me!*

Although K was right about third-graders' crafts projects in general — one wall displayed painted macaroni glued to construction paper to form animal shapes — none of these exhibits included feathers.

The horizontal surfaces were as covered as the walls, with books and papers scattered carelessly across the tops of desks by students following the example of their teacher, whose work station was piled with tumbling stacks of papers held in place with whatever was handy at the moment: a stapler, a brass apple, a dirty coffee cup, a painted rock, a potted plant as brown and crisp as breakfast cereal in a china bowl.

On a table in the far corner of the room I found a cracked aquarium with a rusted screen on top. Inside was a dish of water, a handful of sand, and a seashell from which the stalky eyes of a hermit crab timidly peered out.

The classroom pet, I said to myself, remembering the lop-eared rabbit that had sat so forlornly in a wire cage throughout my kindergarten years, and the ant farm that my first grade teacher had unwittingly cooked when she placed it in a sunny window.

Isn't it bad enough that kids have to be here? I thought. *Why must innocent animals spend their lives in school?*

From the adjacent classroom came the voice of a child.

"Hello," it said.

"Not *hello*," a woman's voice replied crossly. "Not after three-thirty. After three-thirty, thank goodness, it's *goodbye*."

Uh-oh! I thought. I certainly didn't want to be found lurking where I had no good reason to be, so I slipped out of the classroom and high-tailed it home.

With three bright green feathers now in my

possession, far from being satisfied, my curiosity was even more aroused. I sat down on my front steps and laid them side by side on the porch. In the clear, spring sunlight, they sparkled.

Hmmm, I thought. *I wonder what the rest of you looks like?*

Green is not a common color for North American birds. Most, it seems, are gray or black or brown. Some have patches of red or orange or yellow. A few sport blue and purple feathers. But green?

Hummingbirds, perhaps. They're usually green. But a hummingbird with feathers as big as the ones that I'd just found would never get off the ground.

Grackles? They're bigger than hummingbirds, but the dark, shiny green of a grackle is actually much closer to black.

Mallard ducks? Only their tiny head feathers are green.

Finches? Tanagers? Buntings? No, no, and no. The bird that lost these feathers was probably as big as a hawk, with fluorescent green wings and tail.

I was stumped for a logical explanation. Perhaps an illogical one would present itself.

"Are you still brooding about that chicken?" a familiar voice asked.

It was K towering over me.

K is tall. I am not. With her great, long legs and brightly colored clothes, K reminds me of a waterfowl, the kind that strides imperiously through marshes dining on unsuspecting amphibians.

A glint in the eye, a cock of the head, and zap! Gotcha!

K is cuter than most birds, though, with short brown hair, brown eyes, and freckles sprinkled like a constellation across her well-formed nose. And wow, what a mouth! When K smiles, as she was doing now, it spreads all the way across her face.

"Chicken?" I responded. "These feathers aren't from any chicken."

"Of course they are, Fowler," K insisted. "It happens every spring. People buy those baby chicks that have been dyed in the shell, thinking they're so cute and cuddly, that they'll always be fluffy little balls of color running around going peep-peep-peep!"

By way of demonstration, K tucked her thumbs into her underarms, spun in a circle, and flapped her elbows. It was a fascinating performance. I was sorry it was so brief.

"But within a few weeks," K continued, standing over me once again and shaking her finger authoritatively, "those chicks have turned into some very uncute, uncuddly chickens that go poop-poop-poop, and the next thing you know, all that's left of those poor, unfortunate clucks are some brightly colored feathers — feathers no longer attached to anything living, if you get my drift."

"K," I said, exasperated. "You are so wrong!"

"Was this your dime?" she asked, picking up a

coin from my garden and putting it in her pocket.

Sometimes, despite her entertaining appearance, K can be very annoying.

"Keep it," I replied. "Now, if you'll excuse me, I have homework to do."

I stowed my three green feathers in my backpack and went inside, leaving K and her half-baked poultry hypothesis on my front porch. Theory was not what I needed. This was a situation that demanded facts.

It was time to consult Bleeth.

Thurgood Bleeth, Ph.D., is the author of the most valuable book in my library, one that I've owned for many years — more years, in fact, than I've known how to read — a gift from a great-aunt who faithfully sends me books for every gift-giving occasion. Its once-colorful dust jacket long since gone, the hefty, dog-eared volume is titled *Bleeth's Complete Compendium for Boys*.

And complete it truly is! *Bleeth's Compendium* is packed with facts and opinions on virtually every topic under the sun. In my experience, if Thurgood Bleeth can't shed light on the subject, then the subject isn't worth knowing.

The only problem with relying on Bleeth whenever you're stumped for an answer is that Bleeth uses big words where smaller words would do. After a lifetime of exposure to this, I sometimes catch myself talking like him.

With feather in hand, I turned to the chapter headed "Identifying Wildlife." There, just before the section labeled "Footprints," I found "Feathers," a subcategory that Bleeth had thoughtfully organized by color. Intuitively, my eyes landed on "Green."

"There are many green and partially green birds in the world," Bleeth explained in his typically engaging manner, "but for truly spectacular green plumage, nothing is so impressive as parrots *(Psittaciformes)*."

Parrots! I thought. *Of course!*

Eagerly, I continued reading.

"Of the more than three hundred parrots native to Mexico, the Caribbean, Australia, New Zealand, and the jungles of Africa and South America," Bleeth wrote, "green, in all its rich variations, is by far the most prevalent hue. Sadly, the dazzling appearance of these extraordinary birds has been their downfall. Today, many parrot species have become extinct, with others almost certainly doomed to follow, as mankind methodically destroys both bird and habitat in search of decoration and amusement."

I don't know why I didn't consult Bleeth in the first place! Honestly, the man is so knowledgeable that sometimes I wonder if there's ever any need to do any thinking for myself!

For the rest of the evening, I studied Bleeth's recommendations for restoring ecosystems through-out the world. As usual, his ideas were right on the money, but the problem of the world's parrots left me with a feeling of complete and total helplessness.

What, I wondered, *can one sixth-grader do?*

As it turned out, what sixth-graders *should* do is their homework. The next morning, when the other kids turned in their math, social studies, and language arts assignments, I turned up empty-handed. If I squinted at them in just the right way, the zeroes that I earned that day looked like little parrot eggs.

Mrs. Picklestain's Problem

By now, I knew the route like the back of K's head. Three times I'd dared to set foot in the third grade pod, the first by chance, the second from curiosity, and now, this time, to get a firsthand look at what I was hoping would be waiting for me.

The last bell of the day still echoed in my ears. Tired-looking teachers led first-graders by the hand to the buses waiting outside. Other kids, second-graders and third-graders, I guessed, jostled their way toward the exits like so many bowling pins about to fall.

Suddenly, the little kids parted. An older boy dressed in matching red shorts and button-down shirt came trotting like a circus pony down the center of the hall. With one hand, he dragged an overstuffed backpack, soiled and worn, its zipper separating from the fabric. From his other hand dangled a hard black oboe case that banged against his knobby knees with every step.

It was Wallace, the geekiest sixth-grader of them all.

"Hi, Fowler!" he called as he rushed past me.

For some reason, Wallace likes to think that we're friends.

"Goodbye, Wallace," I replied.

Between the nurse's office and the library is the janitor's closet, where Vice President Lloyd now stood untangling an orange extension cord. He nodded to me in recognition. I returned his greeting with a hasty wave.

In the library, the pink-haired woman with big hips was pushing a squeaky metal cart containing a videotape player and stack of tapes. One of the videos tumbled to the floor. Turning her back to me, the pear-shaped matron bent over to retrieve it, an action that had it been out-of-doors would have blocked the sun.

I slipped by unnoticed.

To be certain that the coast was clear, I loitered by a hallway exhibition of third grade wall art. Most of the brightly colored paintings featured spring flowers, all seemingly created by the same clumsy hand. One, however — the only one I liked — appeared to be either a microwave oven or a robot; it was hard to tell which.

It had possibilities.

Having already inspected the first classroom, I cautiously poked my head into the second.

Jackpot!

In the gloom at the back of the room, hanging from the ceiling was a big, black, bell-shaped cage with a motionless shadowy shape inside. Leading to it was a trail of feathers, dozens and dozens of them, mostly long, slightly curved, and green, like the three that had previously found their way to me, but some, including a few drifting in the air, were white, round, and fluffy — down feathers — about the size and shape of popped popcorn.

Making my way past eighteen plastic-topped desks on which eighteen yellow plastic chairs had been upended, I began retrieving the fallen feathers. A few students had failed to put away their notebooks, and from the sloppy cursive handwriting on these, I concluded that I was in the classroom belonging to one Mrs. Picklestain.

Well, Mrs. Picklestain, I thought, stuffing feather after feather into my pocket, *at this rate, I'll soon have enough feathers to make a bird of my very own!*

Once I thought about it, it was obvious, but until I looked inside the big steel cage, I hadn't made the connection: Feathers on the floor are feathers no longer on the bird.

This guy looked terrible! His head, breast, and upper wings were blotched with unsightly bald spots. Half his tail feathers were gone. His beak was scaly.

14

His claws were overgrown, twisted into clumsy hooks. The bottom of his cage was disgusting, as if it hadn't been cleaned for a week or more. The perch on which he glumly sat was chewed and splintered, his water dish was fouled, and there was nothing — not a pellet nor a seed — in the cup that should have held his food.

A combination lock, the kind you'd use to protect your bicycle or the contents of your locker, secured the door to the parrot's cage. When I leaned forward for a closer look, the bird's yellow eyes narrowed into tiny black dots, like those of a wary lizard.

"Hello," he said in a mournful, childlike voice.

"Hello," I answered politely. "How are you?"

"May I help you?" asked an unhelpful, unchildlike voice that suggested the parrot had mastered the art of ventriloquism, for it sounded as if his question were coming from directly behind me.

"I don't think so," I told him. "I was just being curious."

"Well, it's time to take your curiosity home," the stern voice declared. "School is over and my classroom is closed."

I spun around to confront the unforgiving expression of a familiar pear-shaped, pink-haired woman who I instantly concluded must be none other than Mrs. Picklestain.

"S-s-sorry," I stammered. "Wrong room."

A Seed Is Planted

K's mother collects clocks, all kinds of clocks — new ones, old ones, clocks that ding, clocks that bong, clocks that chime out the quarter-hour. In K's house, clocks flaunt themselves from walls, peek from corners, and monopolize tables, shelves, and the fireplace mantelpiece. Curiously, K's mother doesn't bother to synchronize her clocks, so every bell, call, and cuckoo comes as a complete surprise.

One with a sound like that of a distant church bell rang out just as K spoke up.

"How close did you get to this thing?" she asked.

"As close as you can get without being inside the cage," I replied.

"And all these feathers were just lying around on the floor?" she continued, staring at the pile in front of her in disbelief. "You didn't pluck them off the parrot?"

"Actually," I explained, "I was wondering if there might not be a way to stick them back on when I was interrupted by the bird's chief tormentor."

From throughout the room, the soft, steady chorus of ticking clocks supplied a pleasant, restful sound, like crickets singing on a summer night. K let the feathers sift gently through her fingers.

"Perhaps he's sick and Mrs. Picklestain took him to her classroom to nurse him back to health," she suggested.

"Oh, he's sick all right," I said. "But nobody in Mrs. Picklestain's classroom is doing anything to help him. I'm sure that's why he's in such sorry shape. What do third-graders know about taking care of animals?"

"I took care of an animal when I was in third grade," K replied. "Two of them, in fact — guinea pigs. Their names were Fluffy and Muffy. I kept them in a cage in my room."

"Guinea pigs?" I responded in surprise. I'd never known K to have a pet. "What happened to them?"

K's broad mouth descended into a long, elastic frown.

"They died," she said.

Silently, I shook my head from side to side. K's testimony proved my point. Mrs. Picklestain's parrot was in trouble, and it didn't take a houseful of clocks to remind me that he was running out of time.

At that moment, as if it had been reading my mind, a carved walnut clock from which two fat brass weights were suspended chimed once, twice, three times in succession. I looked at my watch. It was four twenty-two.

"If that parrot stays where he is," I observed, "he's a goner."

"What a shame," K said. She inserted a slender green feather into her nut-brown hair, wearing it like a flower. "Maybe somebody should try to rescue him. You know, sneak in and set him free?"

"You mean break into the school?" I responded, astonished.

Such advice seemed quite out of character for K.

"It'd be more like a walk in, actually," she clarified. "Anyway, it's not like what they'd be doing is a crime or anything — unless they got caught, of course."

Suddenly, half a dozen clocks went off all at once, releasing sounds of handbells, buzzers, singing birds, croaking frogs, train whistles, and tinkling bamboo chimes, but none was half as loud as the sound inside my head, where everything seemed to explode, as if fireworks had been launched, with K's impetuous idea being the match that lit the fuse.

Steal the parrot, I said in silence to myself. *Now why didn't I think of that!*

Mulling It Over

Even when it comes from a person who's usually wrong, the power of suggestion can be immense. All weekend long, I thought of nothing but the plight of that miserable, balding bird, and how I might intervene to save him.

Fowler and the Amazing Animal Rescue, I imagined. *Why, it could be a television series!*

In my mind, the theme song played.

What I ate for breakfast remains a mystery,

because my thoughts were about how to get myself in and out of Mrs. Picklestain's classroom undetected. At baseball practice, where Mr. String was helping kids prepare for the City League tryouts, I let strike after strike whiz past me while contemplating the problem of the cage door lock. Saturday evening found me pondering methods for secretly transporting small live animals. And at bedtime, I tossed and turned for hours, grappling with the long, strong arms of my conscience.

Could I really do such a thing? I fretted.

On Sunday morning I went to church, where after an unnerving sermon about the Ten Commandments, I spotted K and her mother headed for the parking lot.

"K, wait up," I called. "I need to ask you something."

K turned and looked in my direction. Her eyes landed on a folded dollar bill that had blown into the bushes. Like a great blue heron spearing a minnow, she retrieved it in a single stroke.

"Is that your money?" I asked her.

"It is now," she replied.

"Somebody probably meant to put that in the collection plate," I observed.

"Don't be silly, Fowler," she said. "The collection plate is inside."

K turned away to join her mother. I hurried to keep up with her long-legged stride.

"Was there something else you wanted?" she asked.

"Listen," I said, "you've known me for a long time. Do you see me as the kind of person who deliberately breaks the rules?"

K stood beside her mother's car and looked me squarely in the eye. In the bright morning light, I could make out the shape of every freckle on her nose. No two were alike.

"Fowler," K said with a carefree toss of her head, "your problem is that you think too much."

By Sunday afternoon, I realized that setting free a sickly jungle creature in the middle of a busy North American city would not be doing him any favors. No, if I were to liberate him, I would have to care for him. But where, I wondered, could I put him? How do you keep a full-grown parrot hidden from everyone you know?

No matter how many times I recirculated the questions, I found no satisfactory answers.

Finally, that night, my mind spent and the weekend gone, I had to face facts: the situation was hopeless. Breaking and entering, burglary, kidnapping, possessing stolen property, providing unlicensed veterinary services — such activities were beyond my capabilities. K may have set a noble goal, but this mission was impossible. I couldn't do it and that was that.

My decision made, I closed my eyes and surrendered my cares to the comforting caresses of sleep.

A Personal Plea

I arrived at school Monday morning just as Vice President Lloyd was raising the American flag. An older, slightly stooped man with thick bifocal glasses, he seemed to enjoy his work as elementary school custodian. The title that he chose to go by — vice president — had nothing to do with his present position but was a holdover from his previous career in advertising, where apparently he had been some sort of big shot.

"That title was the only part of my job that mattered," I once overheard him telling Mr. String.

Except for Vice President Lloyd, a couple of day-care kids, and the occasional teacher suffering from insomnia, few people came to school this early.

"Good morning," Vice President Lloyd called out cheerfully as the colorful symbol of freedom fluttered in the spring breeze. "Great day to be alive, isn't it?"

"Uh, sure," I answered. But no sooner had I spoken than my inner voice intruded.

Unless you're locked up in a black steel cage, it said. *In which case, this day could be your last.*

Forget it! my common sense replied. *There's nothing you can do!*

Once inside the schoolhouse door, however, my feet turned toward the third grade pod.

No, no! I warned. *This won't work!*

By then my legs had joined the conspiracy. Before I could protest any further, I found myself standing in the now-familiar hallway of concrete-block walls littered with rows of lookalike flower paintings.

From the first classroom, a rustle followed by a sneeze suggested that the messy teacher was already at her post. I tiptoed past the entry and slipped into Mrs. Picklestain's darkened classroom as silently as a feather falling to the floor.

My eyes surveyed the gloom. Ominously, like a rope swinging from a gallows, the black cage swayed from a hook in the ceiling. Outlined against the curved steel bars was the unmoving silhouette of a parrot.

There's nothing you can do! my common sense repeated.

You could at least see if he's still alive, my inner voice replied.

The parrot seemed to perk up when he saw me.

"Hello," he said.

"Hello," I whispered in reply.

Since the time I'd seen it before, his cage still hadn't been cleaned, but his water had been changed, and there were a couple of seeds at the bottom of his food dish. The parrot himself, however, looked even worse. The bare patches on his body were so ugly that for a moment I turned my head away.

"Hello," he said again.

"Is that all you can say?" I asked.

Talk about your small talk! For an animal whose fame is based on its verbal ability, this bird sure had a limited vocabulary.

"Hello, hello," he repeated, looking down at me mournfully. "Hello, hello, hello."

"My name is Fowler," I told him. "It's not the greatest name in the world, but somehow, it's the name I got. If you want to talk to me, you'll have to use it."

"Hello," the parrot said.

"Not hello," I replied. "It's Fowler."

"Hello," he said.

"Fowler," I repeated. "F-O-W-L-E-R. Now say it: Fowler."

"Hello," he said.

"This conversation isn't going anywhere," I replied. "But I am. I have to get to class. I just dropped by to see how you're doing."

The parrot shook his head rapidly back and forth, like a person indicating, "No." He hopped over to his water cup and raked his beak up and down against it.

This must be how they keep their beaks so sharp, I thought.

"Well, I'll leave you to your work," I announced. "So long, now."

"Hello!" he cried, followed by an ear-splitting screech. "*AAAWK!* Hello, hello, hello!"

"Shhh!" I responded. "Keep your voice down! You'll get me in trouble!"

"*AAAWK!* Hello, hello, hello, hello!" he continued, flapping wildly about his cage. This was not a smart move, since even more feathers flew from his sad, scrawny body.

One of these feathers was extraordinarily beautiful. The bottom half was a phosphorescent yellow-green, the top half a deep ruby red. I reached between the dull black bars to pick it up. That was when I saw it — not the feather, but the message — a word composed of scratches on his water cup. Slashed by the razor tip of the parrot's pointed beak, the marks were crudely formed, but unmistakable.

H-A-L-P, it said.

HALP? I thought. *What's HALP?*

Then it hit me. No doubt, the ailing bird had intended to write "HELP," but in his haste, he'd gotten one letter wrong.

You could have knocked me over with a feather! Was this parrot actually asking me to help him?

"Lorna, do you have any extra glue sticks?" a girlish voice inquired. "Someone left the caps off mine and now they're completely dried up."

Uh-oh! I thought.

It was the teacher from the neighboring classroom.

"Oh, I'm sorry," she said. "I was expecting to find Mrs. Picklestain."

"Uh, so was I," I blurted out. "But since she's not here, I'll just be going."

"Whom shall I say dropped by?" she asked as I nervously backed down the hall.

"I'm ummm . . . ummm . . ."

Frantically, I tried to think of something, but all my anxious head could come up with were beads of sweat.

"Are you sure you're in the right place?" the teacher inquired.

"He's with me," a voice announced. Unexpectedly materializing like a housecat from hiding, Vice President Lloyd stood in the hallway, a pair of red rubber-handled pliers in his hand. "Tell Mrs. Picklestain we fixed the outlet behind her desk," he said. "It was just a loose wire."

"All right," the teacher replied. "I'll be sure to let her know."

A Plan Is Hatched

Why other people do the things they do, I'm sure I'll never understand. Usually, it's someone's thick-headed, selfish action that bewilders me. In the case of Vice President Lloyd, however, I found myself taken aback by what appeared to be an act of kindness. Why should he fib to Mrs. Picklestain on my account?

"Thanks," I said, hitching up my backpack.

"Don't mention it," the aging custodian replied.

Whatever his reason for helping me, it was clear that Vice President Lloyd wasn't inclined to talk about it now. He'd already switched on his floor buffer. As he turned his back to me to polish an already very shiny floor, I set off for the sixth grade wing.

The mystery of the custodian's intervention faded as I thought about the beak-scrawled plea of Mrs. Picklestain's parrot. In desperation, the one-word wonder had scribbled a misspelled cry for assistance and addressed it to me. Though I tried to concentrate on classwork, the plaintive image of his hasty "HALP" wouldn't go away. Without my realizing it was happening, this parrot problem had become personal.

How could I say no?

"There isn't a moment to lose," I announced to K at lunch. "Time's a-wasting."

"I'm sure that's true, Fowler," K replied, "but if you eat too fast, you'll only get hiccups. Trust me, I know."

"You don't understand," I said. "What I mean is,

it's now or never. We have to make our move, and fast!"

Perplexed, K turned her brown eyes to the ceiling. No sooner did she look away than Wallace, dressed in what I could have sworn was a sailor suit, clambered in to take the seat beside her. With a clatter that sent a salt shaker tumbling into my lap, Wallace dropped both his metal lunch box and his oboe case onto the table.

"Hi, guys!" he called out cheerfully. "What's up?"

Ignoring the intrusion, I leaned across the table and whispered to K, improvising a code in case Wallace should overhear.

"It's about the prisoner," I said. "You know — flap, flap?"

More confused than ever and dismayed by the turn her lunch break had taken, K's eyes darted around the room in search of less peculiar company.

"What are you talking about, Fowler?" she demanded.

Obviously, K had forgotten our discussion about Mrs. Picklestain's parrot.

Maybe it's just as well, I figured. *I probably should work alone.*

"Nothing, K," I answered. "I was just wondering if you'd like some of my fries."

K looked at me distrustfully.

"You haven't had them in your mouth, have you, Fowler?" she asked. "The ends look sort of gummy."

From the seat beside her, the whiny voice of Wallace butted in. "If she doesn't want them," he volunteered, "I do."

That afternoon, the plaintive parrot still on my mind, I flung my backpack into the living room closet and dashed upstairs to map out a plan. My problem, I realized, was that I'd been looking at this thing all wrong. I'd been fretting over the bird's predicament from the point of view of a law-abiding citizen. No wonder I wasn't able to help him. Desperate situations call for desperate solutions.

Well, no more Mr. Nice Guy! I thought.

The way I saw it, getting into Mrs. Picklestain's classroom wasn't an issue — I'd done that twice already — but getting the cage door open was. There were other major obstacles, as well.

I made a list.

One, I wrote, *opening the lock.*

Two, getting the bird out of the school.

Three, keeping the bird out of sight.

I studied what I'd written down so far. My inner voice prompted me to add another entry.

Four, getting away with it.

This, I concluded, could prove to be the biggest stumbling block of all. Already, three people had seen me lurking around Mrs. Picklestain's domain: the pink-haired Mrs. Picklestain herself, the third grade teacher from the adjacent classroom, and the strangely helpful school custodian, Vice President

Lloyd. If the bird suddenly were missing, it would be simply a matter of time before one of these grownups thought of me. Why, I'd have to be a complete doofus to think that I could escape suspicion!

I've got to hand it to my brain. What a well-oiled machine it is! No sooner did I think of the word *doofus* than it occurred to me my plan could work.

All I needed was another suspect! Someone more likely to have committed the crime than me; someone known throughout the school for his peculiar, inexplicable behavior; someone who looks as if his mother dressed him; someone who is never without a satchel-shaped container that, incidentally, is exactly the right size for smuggling an undernourished parrot; someone whose best friend is an oboe! I would find a way to lay the blame on the unsuspecting — nay, clueless — Wallace!

I clapped my hands together in excitement. From the desk top, my list fluttered to the floor, landing upside down at my feet. I read it from where I stood, last entry first.

Four, it said, *getting away with it.*

Check, I thought.

Three, keeping the bird out of sight.

Hmmm, I mused. *I guess he can live in my closet. I'll just have to clean it up a little to make room.*

Two, getting the bird out of the school.

For this, I would use Wallace's oboe case. I'd only need it for a little while.

Check, I thought.

I turned my attention to the last item on the list, which was, in fact, the first.

One, opening the lock.

Here, I had to admit that I was stumped. But experience long ago taught me that when truly stumped, the solution that never fails is Thurgood Bleeth, Ph.D. I stepped to my bookshelf and removed the invaluable *Bleeth's Complete Compendium for Boys,* flipping quickly to the chapter concerning things that start with the letter L.

"Locks," Dr. Bleeth observed, "are useless without keys or combinations, and this is their fatal weakness."

That Bleeth, I thought. *He's so insightful.*

"If something is important enough to lock away," I continued reading, "it is equally important that its owner be able to retrieve it on demand. Thus, people hide keys and written combinations in places that are easy for them to access. Unfortunately, such hidey-holes are also easily discovered by others."

Or fortunately, I thought, *depending on how you look at it.*

Bleeth, of course, was way ahead of me.

"According to a survey of successful criminals," he wrote, "the most popular spot for hiding keys and important scraps of paper is the middle desk drawer. This is followed closely by the underwear drawer in the bureau, the medicine cabinet, the freezer, and decorative objects in plain sight, such as vases, pottery, and cookie jars."

I'll have to remember this, I thought.

Bleeth, however, wasn't finished. "Books are also handy places for secreting short messages and small objects," he wrote, "and sometimes, especially among the more dimwitted, keys and combinations can be found affixed to the very objects they're meant to protect. Just remember, most people are not very clever. The moral? Seek, and ye shall find."

Grateful to be once again so well informed, I shut the book.

There it is, I thought, *a plan!*

All I had to do now was search Mrs. Picklestain's classroom, borrow an oboe case, hide the parrot in my closet, and blame the whole nefarious caper on Wallace.

All in all, I had to admit, it had been a productive afternoon.

A Date with Destiny

When officials of the United States government made up their minds to put men on the moon, they first gave themselves a deadline, and then they rushed around like crazy figuring out how to meet it. Few people thought they would succeed, but history bears witness to their wisdom.

If you want to accomplish something that's never been done before, *when* always comes before *how.*

For Parrot Liberation Day, I chose Thursday, a date just forty-eight hours away. Obviously, I needed a certain amount of time to work out the details, but I was concerned about the beleaguered bird's ability to hold on any longer. Furthermore, Thursday was the day of the City League baseball tryouts, which were to be held at the school. These, I reasoned, could provide a helpful diversion. Still another reason for my haste was that now that I had momentum, I didn't want to lose my edge. That edge is the criminal's greatest ally.

The criminal's second greatest ally is the patsy — also known as the scapegoat. This is an unwitting bystander whom the criminal sets up to take the fall. To put this piece of the plan into place involved risking my social status. Let's face it: People who hang out with geeks are often presumed to be geeks themselves. I could wind up losing every friend I had!

I figured I'd better lay the groundwork with K.

Since I was sort of staying at her house until one or the other of my parents returned, there was no need to knock. Her mother sidetracked me with a peanut butter and jelly sandwich, but eventually I found K in her room dropping coins into a five-gallon water jug that she keeps in a corner beside her chest of drawers. The jug was more than three-fourths full of money.

"My gosh, K," I said. "You must have five hundred dollars in there."

"Probably," she agreed.

"Shouldn't you put it in the bank?" I asked.

"I like to look at it," K replied. "At the bank, they don't let you look at your money."

A cuckoo clock chirped a single tweet. I found K's accidental fortune interesting, but at that moment, it wasn't foremost on my mind. I made a stab at changing the subject.

"You know, K," I said, "I may not be the coolest guy in school, but I've been very careful over the years to avoid being the nerdiest."

"That you have, Fowler," K agreed.

She smiled in friendly approval. Her brown eyes formed tiny, crinkly lines at the edges.

Do mine do that? I wondered.

"I've always paid attention to the prevailing hairstyles," I went on, "and when the craze was at its peak, I had an enviable collection of trading cards."

"I remember that, Fowler," K said, releasing coins one after another into the jug. "You spent all your allowance on them. Then you tried to borrow money from me to get more."

"I just wanted to be one of the guys, K," I explained.

"Whatever," K replied.

I continued my confession. "I've participated enthusiastically in every popular sport," I said, "even the ones that I find boring. For two years now, I've been a relief pitcher for the Superior Limestone Rockets in the City League. Many is the time I've spent sitting around waiting for my turn."

"You're a real team player, Fowler. Everybody knows that," K affirmed.

"And when, for no apparent reason," I said, "everybody suddenly switched from wearing shirts with the trademark of a shoe company to shirts with the name of a store, I was right there with them."

"You definitely keep up with things, Fowler, I'll give you that," K observed. "Nobody could ever accuse you of being out of step."

"Thank you, K," I said sincerely. "No matter what happens, I'd like you to remember that. It's very important to me."

"All right, Fowler," K agreed. "I will."

I left her to her counting and went back to my house. Despite K's assurances, it was hard for me to dial the number that I found in the school directory. My hands shook with anxiety.

"You've reached the Wilsons'," voices sang into my unprepared ear, "but we're not here, so leave your number, for us to hear."

Good grief! I thought, recoiling at the ridiculous recording. Not only had Wallace and his parents performed their message as an a capella family chorus, the only rhyme they could come up with was "here" with "hear." Clearly, Wallace's geek problem was inherited. Only the traumatic image of a half-green, half-flesh-colored bird weakly pecking at death's door persuaded me to swallow my pride and leave a message.

"Wallace," I said. "This is Fowler. If you'd like to be on a baseball team with me, meet me at the practice field tomorrow after school."

I hung up the phone. Oddly, I felt a surge of relief. The die was cast. There was no turning back. I'd just granted his fondest wish to a person born wearing a great big KICK ME sign, and I'd done it while coldly planning for him to be blamed for my bird-napping.

This was it. I'd taken my first premeditated step along the criminal path.

Step aside, world! I thought. *There's a new kid in town!*

My Friend Wallace

What I know about oboes you could fit into a parrot's beak, but oboe cases, now that's another story. Many is the time I'd witnessed Wallace stumbling into class clutching his absurd valise.

Only slightly smaller than the average table lamp, Wallace's oboe case was made of a metal shell with a black, leatherlike finish. Two gleaming silver latches held it securely closed. Had he had sense enough to leave well enough alone, the appearance of his oboe case might not have been so bad, but Wallace, being Wallace, had customized it with stickers, dozens of them, depicting airplanes, dinosaurs, and roly-poly kittens, handouts that he'd received while sitting beside his mother as she drove through the drive-through at the bank.

In my opinion, he might as well have tied a pink ribbon around it, because Wallace's oboe case looked just like a carrying case for dolls.

At the baseball practice fields, I found the oboe case standing on its end with its owner balanced on top, scraping his foot in the dust, patiently waiting for me to arrive.

"Am I late?" I asked.

School couldn't have been out for more than five minutes.

"I got excused an hour early," Wallace explained. "I didn't want to miss you."

"Holy smokes, Wallace," I remarked.

Wallace stood up. He was wearing a shorts and shirt outfit that imitated a Major League baseball uniform — pin-striped, collarless, with a number printed on the back — the kind that little kids wear for pajamas. As if this weren't bad enough, on Wallace's feet were open-toed sandals. I shook my head in disbelief.

"Did you bring any equipment?" I asked.

"I brought a glove," he answered.

Wallace picked up a brand new, black leather fielder's glove, a signature model with double-stitching, palm reinforcement, and a full basket web. It must have set his parents back a hundred bucks.

Hmmm, I thought, tossing him a baseball which he bobbled, but did not drop.

"Good catch, Wallace," I said encouragingly. "Have you ever played baseball before?"

"I've always wanted to," he replied.

For the next half-hour or so, I hit grounders and pop flies to the geeky rookie until it was obvious that he was no worse than lots of other kids. Then I showed him how to run the bases and demonstrated my special technique for sliding into home. To his credit, he was an attentive student.

"By the way, Wallace," I said, handing him a silver bat. "Do you always carry your oboe with you?"

Wallace cast his eyes toward the empty bleachers where the oboe case sat unattended and ominous, like a package left by a mad bomber.

"I have to, Fowler," the lanky little loser confessed. "I have lessons every day, plus a recital coming up. Have you ever been in a recital?"

"That'll be the day!" I said with a hearty laugh.

I wound up and delivered my fastest, trickiest pitch, the not-yet-famous Fowler knuckleball, the one I call the City League Equalizer.

WHOOSH!

Instead of shifting his weight forward like every

batter knows you're supposed to do, the novice Wallace jumped back, closed his eyes, and swung the big metal bat with all the power his spindly arms could muster.

BONG!

Like a sledgehammer driving the golden spike to complete America's transcontinental railroad, Wallace's bat connected with the baseball, sending it over my head, over second base, beyond the outfield, and into the trees that separated the school practice field from the subdivision beyond. No one but no one had ever hit the ball that far before. I'm not sure, but I think I heard it break a window.

"Good grief, Wallace!" I exclaimed. "You might have killed someone!"

"I'm sorry," Wallace responded meekly. "I thought the ball was going to hit me."

The Moment Arrives

On Parrot Liberation Day, the bathtub overflowed.

I'd left it running while I went next door to borrow a clean towel, arriving just as K's mother was placing breakfast on the table.

Such a catastrophe could not be considered a good omen, so while mopping up the mess, I convinced myself that signs and premonitions were superstitious nonsense. I would focus on the mission that lay ahead. After all, a bird's life was at stake — an issue much more important than household plumbing.

More bad news awaited me at school. Mr. String, it seems, had been serious about the latest homework assignment. He handed me a blank sheet of paper on which he'd scrawled my name followed by a big, red, and increasingly familiar zero.

Ouch! I thought.

Lunchtime was no better. The cafeteria ran out of pizza just as it was my turn. The only thing left was chef's salad. With a flimsy plastic fork, I sifted the tasteless mixture in hopes of uncovering something that I could eat. Sitting beside me, K popped a savory circle of thin-sliced pepperoni into her mouth.

"You're unusually quiet today, Fowler," she observed, recovering a runaway strand of mozzarella cheese with her fingertip. "What's the matter? Cat got your tongue?"

"I keep thinking I've forgotten something," I answered, "but I can't remember what it is."

"Of course not," K purred sympathetically, patting me on the arm. Her fingertips left a smudge of oily tomato sauce just above my wrist. Pretending to be checking my watch, I discreetly ducked my head beneath the table and licked it.

At the water fountain, where I've safely slurped a thousand times without incident, I misjudged the distance and hit the metal spigot with my nose. The pain was awful, but thankfully brief, and while it didn't appear to do any permanent damage — just a small, purple bruise — I had to report to the nurse for the usual paperwork.

The only other thing that happened was that I sat on gum, but that's not particularly unusual. I was able to pick most of it off during math class.

With the tolling of the last bell, the moment that I'd waited for was suddenly upon me. I could feel my lungs expanding. I could feel my heart beating faster. I could feel something tugging annoyingly at my sleeve.

"I'm so excited," Wallace said, scampering in circles like a puppy. "Look, I got those shoes you told me to."

Wallace held his right foot up for me to see. He was wearing the finest baseball cleats that money could buy.

"Holy smokes, Wallace!" I exclaimed. "I thought only professionals could afford shoes like that!"

"I didn't want to let you down," he explained.

I changed into my battered, dusty bargain cleats and gathered up my well-worn glove and bat from my locker. This would be my third year on the Rockets, so unless I simply failed to show up, for me, the tryouts were merely a formality. Wallace, on the other hand, was about to learn the facts of life the hard way.

This, my inner voice reminded me, could not be helped. It was a matter of balance, the inevitable outcome of a timeless equation: For every successful act of crime, there must be a victim.

"Here, Wallace," I said, giving him the baseball gear. "You carry this stuff. I'll carry your oboe case."

"Gee, thanks, Fowler," he said.

"Don't mention it," I replied. "I really mean that."

Just as I'd expected, the practice field was crowded. Kids from all over were queuing up, anxious to take their shot at being a player on a real, no-nonsense baseball team. Leaving the oboe case underneath the bleachers, I helped Wallace fill out an application, and together we took our place in line.

There must be fifty ways to organize a group — by size, by years of experience, by date of birth, by the time of arrival, to name just a few examples — but for some reason, the people in charge of schools have cast their lot with the alphabet. If your last name starts with A, B, or C, you'll always be among the first to eat, the first to be seated, and the first to be called to perform. If yours is near the end of the alphabet, where names such as Wallace Wilson and Fowler Young are found, you wait. Such a system is either a mindless habit or proof of the power of librarians.

"It could be an hour before we get our turn," I complained.

"I don't mind," Wallace said. "I've already waited for years. What's a few more minutes to a kid like me?"

"That's very philosophical of you, Wallace," I replied, "but some of us have other things to do. So if you don't mind, hold our place in line while I go make a phone call. Okay?"

"Sure," the little sap agreed. "No problem."

It should take no more than five minutes to spring the parrot, race home, toss him into my closet, plant some incriminating feathers in Wallace's oboe case, and return, I figured, but even if it took twice that long, I was certain no one would notice my absence. After all, baseball was in the air!

The oboe case was right where I'd left it. No one was around to see me pick it up and dash to the school. My plan was going like clockwork.

This is almost too easy! I mused.

At the building entrance, the flag had been taken down for the evening. A yellow pickup truck, apparently abandoned, sat at the far end of the parking lot. The school building itself — a long, low, brown brick structure with only an occasional window — was quiet.

And its big, steel front doors were locked up tight!

Dang! I thought. *I didn't count on this!*

With panic rising within me, I hurried to the side of the building.

Maybe they forgot one, I said to myself.

The entrance to the gym was locked. Ditto for the one to the cafeteria. At the back of the school, where

42

the door is tucked away in an alcove, I noisily rattled the handle up and down while pushing firmly with my shoulder. It was no use. The door stood fast.

Dang and double dang! I thought. *This is like trying to open a rock!*

Discouraged, I picked up Wallace's oboe case with its embarrassing baby stickers and trudged all the way around the building, through the playground, past the bicycle stands, around the concrete picnic tables, and underneath the PTO memorial tree, searching in vain for an open window.

It's not like trying to open a rock, I corrected myself. *It's like trying to open a tomb. Because inside, a parrot lies dying.*

Back at the main entrance, frustrated by events, worried about the bird, and angry with myself for not factoring a locked schoolhouse into my rescue plan, I threw Wallace's oboe case against the door.

BLAM!

I must be a magnet for the unexpected. What happened next was as if the building had suddenly succumbed to a magic spell. Yielding to the impact of the flying case, the front door swung smoothly open, as though guided by an invisible doorman's inviting hand.

Amazed by this sudden change of fortune, I quickly thanked my lucky stars, and without looking back hurried inside.

No Time to Lose

Mrs. Picklestain's parrot was sitting in the litter pan on the bottom of the cage.

"Hello," he sighed.

"I've come to get you out of here," I explained. "Do you have any idea where Mrs. Picklestain keeps the combination?"

"Hello," the parrot repeated.

"Oh, for heaven's sake," I muttered, jerking open Mrs. Picklestain's middle desk drawer.

Mrs. Picklestain must have taught school for many years, I concluded, for stuffed into her desk was a vast, disorderly collection of not-quite-useless items, and other soon-to-be-obsolete stuff. I sifted through pennies, paper clips, peppermints, plastic buttons, and metal badges bearing slogans such as IF YOU CAN READ THIS, THANK A TEACHER and I ♥ WOODWINDS. There were many, many scraps of paper — excuses for being absent, memos from the principal to the staff, a typewritten grocery list with what I supposed was meant to be milk inexplicably spelled M-I-L-T. None bore the numbers I was searching for.

"Hello," the parrot groaned.

"I'm working on it," I replied.

I dumped a vase of flowers into the wastebasket, stagnant water and all. No combination was hidden within. From the baseball fields, a cheer went up.

I'd better hurry, I thought.

I flipped through Mrs. Picklestain's reference books, upended her lamp, and inspected the bottom of her jumbo jar of hand cream. I took every tissue from her two-hundred-fifty-count Kleenex box, pulled the bottom off her three-hole punch, examined the battery in her commemorative clock, and removed from its frame a snapshot of Mrs. Picklestain shaking hands with a state representative. Striking out, I shifted my search from Mrs. Picklestain's desk to the parrot's cage.

"Hello," he gasped.

The parrot's repetitious greeting had become a dreadful, desperate sound. It wasn't so much a word as it was a hiss, like air escaping from a balloon, or a dying man giving up the ghost. I spun the graduated wheel on the lock, first to the left, then to the right.

Perhaps random numbers will work, I thought.

The lock refused to open. By now, the parrot lay on his back with his feet up in the air. They looked like miniature trees in winter.

"Hello," he wheezed.

The commotion out at the practice field intensified. I could hear people hollering and clapping. Some were shouting, "Go, go, go!"

Where did that woman hide the combination? I asked myself.

I needed the answer, and fast. Time was running

out, for both the parrot and me. Forcefully, I shook the lock.

For every action, explains *Bleeth's Complete Compendium for Boys,* there is an equal but opposite reaction. Lock shaking, it turns out, is an excellent demonstration of this principle. The parrot's cage, suspended from the ceiling, immediately swung away from me, which caused the litter pan to slide out and fly into the air. With a great, reverberating clatter, the metal disc struck the floor, where it landed on its edge and spun around and around like an oversized coin, before coming to rest upside down amid the pellets, paper, and parrot poop now scattered from one end of Mrs. Picklestain's classroom to the other.

That was when I found what I was looking for.

I don't know how he does it, but once again, Bleeth was as right as rain. The dotty Mrs. Picklestain had stuck the secret combination to the very object she'd intended to protect! Scotch-taped to the bottom of the litter pan was an index card on which her aged hand had penned three shaky numbers: 15, 14, 22.

Within seconds, I had the cage door open. The parrot, who'd scrambled for higher ground when the litter pan became airborne, now dangled from the cage by his foot. Wasting no more time, I scooped him up. The unfortunate creature, consisting of little more than feathers, beak, and trembling bones, was nearly weightless in my hand.

"It's okay," I reassured him. "You'll soon be free."

Using one hand, I flipped up the latches of Wallace's oboe case, and with the toe of my baseball cleats, shoved it open.

Knowledge is power, they say, so ignorance, it follows, is a system-wide power failure. What I didn't know about oboes was brought home to me at the same moment that the parrot clamped his beak around my finger.

"Yow!" I cried, dropping the fearsome feather duster to the floor.

Contrary to what I'd expected, Wallace's oboe case wasn't hollow. Instead of being nice and roomy inside, like a suitcase, it was filled with solid foam that had been sculpted to fit the pipe-shaped parts of an oboe as snug as a bug in a tapestry. There wasn't room for anything else — not a hummingbird, not a wren, not a finch, and most especially not a parrot who's roughly the size of a crow.

How was I to know? I wondered to myself. *I'm not a musician!*

With mounting anxiety, I considered this new setback. If it were closed up in Wallace's oboe case, a parrot such as the one now waddling around on Mrs. Picklestain's classroom floor would immediately be smashed flat as a tortilla. My plan was coming unraveled.

Trouble follows trouble. From the direction of the library came the distinctive whine of Vice President Lloyd's electric floor buffer.

I've got to get out of here! I said to myself.

Meanwhile, the parrot, in that comical, drunken stagger so characteristic of his species, was headed for the doorway as fast as the nearly dead can go.

By now, my heart was beating a mile a minute, sweat was pouring from my brow, and panic was overtaking me, nearly silencing my inner voice.

Do something! it gasped. *Improvise!*

I cast my eyes around Mrs. Picklestain's classroom. The place was a shambles. Books, tissues, contents of drawers, and unidentifiable particles from the bottom of the birdcage lay everywhere.

Who could have done such a thing? I thought. *Surely, not me!*

Spying the empty Kleenex box, I picked it up, intercepted the parrot just as he was about to enter the hallway, and stuffed the dumbfounded creature inside. At nine and a half inches long, a Kleenex box is not a comfortable fit for a twelve-inch parrot, but if you're careful and fold the tail feathers back, it'll do.

Anyway, I thought, *what choice do I have?*

The parrot now packaged for travel, I located Wallace's oboe case, ran like the prairie wind all the way home, dashed madly up the stairs, jerked the bird from the box like a rabbit from a hat, and tossed him unceremoniously into my bedroom closet, where earlier I'd set out food and water.

"I'll be back as soon as I can," I told him, turning

on the closet light. "Make yourself at home."

Excitement surged through me like lightning bolts through Dr. Frankenstein's monster. My mind was churning and so were my legs. Stumbling down the stairs, I froze when my hand reached the doorknob.

"Uh-oh!" I cried.

Like a greyhound rounding the end of a track, I skidded through a change of direction, took the stairs two at a time, tore open my dresser drawer, and snatched up a handful of green feathers, which I stuffed around the instrument parts in Wallace's oboe case.

"Sorry, Wallace," I said with a chuckle so evil-sounding it startled me, "but the picture is not complete without the frame."

The Rookie

Nothing *ever* goes according to plan! Have I mentioned this?

They say that life is full of surprises, but I say it's more than that. Life is perpetual surprise. From beginning to end, it's just one long encounter with the unexpected. Each day we ricochet like a pinball from BOO! to OOPS! to WATCH OUT! until one day, when we're least expecting it, it's over.

Perhaps it's no use even *having* a plan. Perhaps plans formed by the mind of man will always be at odds with those of the higher powers.

With time slipping away at the baseball tryouts, I burst through my front door only to encounter K coming up the steps.

"Hey, Fowler," she greeted me, bending over to pick up two dimes and a nickel that no doubt recently had been mine. "How's it going?"

I screeched to a halt so quickly that I imagined smoke rising from my cleats.

"Good grief, K," I exclaimed, "you startled me!"

"Is that Wallace's oboe?" she asked. "For a second there, I thought you were carrying a purse."

I looked at the object that had caught her eye. A bright green feather was sticking from the lid. With the deftness of a skilled pickpocket, I plucked it free and closed my hand around it.

"Are you all right, Fowler?" K inquired. "You seem awfully jumpy."

"Me, jumpy?" I responded, shifting my gaze to the streetlight beyond K's head. "It's just that I'm late for tryouts, that's all," I explained. "I'll have to talk to you later."

"There's more to life than sports, Fowler," K called as I raced down the sidewalk. "Just remember that."

At the practice field, nearly everyone was gone. I was too late! The tryouts were over. The only people remaining were a few parent volunteers packing folding tables and stowing baseball gear in minivans, and Wallace, of course, sitting on the bleachers looking as happy as a clam in the briny blue sea.

"Fowler, where've you been?" he called. "You missed everything!"

"Something came up," I replied lamely, handing him his instrument case.

"Oh, thanks," he said. "I completely forgot that I have a lesson."

"You have a lesson every day, Wallace," I pointed out.

"I can't remember anything right now," he explained. "I'm so excited! Did you see me hit the ball? I did it with my eyes open this time, just like you said, and oh, Fowler, I made the team! I'm a Rocket! How can I ever thank you? You're the best friend a guy ever had!"

With that, the little loser hugged me.

"Wait a minute!" I cried, pushing him away. "You mean, you're on the team and I'm not? How can that be?"

Wallace stared at me, just as I, on so many other occasions, have stared in bewilderment at him.

"Are you okay, Fowler?" he asked. "You look a little green."

I trudged home, pausing now and then to shake my head. I could hardly believe what had happened. I know that we're supposed to pay for our sins someday, but I'd always thought "someday" meant later on in life. I had no idea that the higher powers would try to settle the score so promptly.

With so many things going wrong, I was especially apprehensive about what I'd find waiting for me at home. Tiptoeing up the stairs, I slowly cracked opened the door to my closet and peeked inside.

Is he dead? I wondered.

Mrs. Picklestain's former parrot not only was still among the living, he was swinging happily on a coat hanger, munching on a peanut. He greeted me with an ear-splitting screech.

"AAAWK!"

"Shhh!" I told him. "Keep your voice down!"

From the looks of the place, the parrot had been having a grand old time, celebrating the caged-bird version of Thanksgiving. Even in the jungle, it's doubtful that a parrot sees so much food. In anticipation of his arrival, I'd set out a bowl of kiwi fruit, mangoes, and bananas, spread peanut butter on crackers, and filled a cup with mixed nuts. On a dinner plate I'd placed two slices of whole wheat toast, a handful of leftover pizza crusts, a chopped hard-boiled egg, and a bunch of fat, purple grapes. For dessert there were sunflower seeds. To be sure he wasn't missing any essential micronutrients, I'd squirted vitamins into his drinking water. Since good health also depends on exercise, where my clothes once hung I'd rigged a parrot playground from wooden coat hangers, a rope, a long dangling chain, and a bell. On the floor below I'd spread out the morning newspaper — a sensible precaution under any circumstances, but especially helpful now, given the animal's sudden change in diet. In short, although I was sure I had a lot to learn about taking care of parrots, I'd tried to think of everything.

One thing, however, I hadn't thought of — a name for my new houseguest. It's likely that Mrs. Picklestain and her third-graders had given him one, but whatever that name may have been, I felt that I must change it, if for no other reason than to obscure the trail of evidence linking me to the crime.

What's a good name for a parrot? I asked myself.

Polly?

No, too common.

Squawko?

Too stupid.

Raskolnikov?

Too hard to pronounce.

Taco, Chalupa, Burrito, Gordita?

I must be getting hungry.

Then my inner voice advised me that at last I had the opportunity to do what somebody should have done a dozen years before. With a single, well-chosen word, I could set things right.

And so it came to pass that I gave my parrot an ordinary name, a friendly, memorable, nickname-only name — a name such as one that I, Fowler Fillmore Young, had been denied.

"Hello, Jack," I said.

"Hello," Jack replied, followed by a screech so loud it shook my brain. *"AAAAAAAAAWK!"*

Covering My Tracks

It was my first major crime, and, like a parrot forgotten in his cage, I'd made quite a mess of it.

Witnesses had observed me casing Mrs. Picklestain's room. Others could connect me to Wallace's feather-filled oboe case. At the very moment the crime was being committed, dozens of people knew I wasn't where I was supposed to be. As for the crime scene itself, there was little left in that disastrous mess that did not now bear my finger-prints. Covering my tracks would not be easy.

A life of crime, however, is based on a kind of faith, and every person who chooses to become a criminal is, at heart, an optimist — unwavering, steadfast, resolute — the sort of person who, even when standing underneath the hangman's noose, believes he's still got a chance — a good chance — to get away with it. Anyway, I reminded myself, it's not as if I had actually been *seen* taking the parrot from Mrs. Picklestain's classroom.

Let them suspect me! I thought defiantly. *Suspicion alone is not sufficient to convict!*

The way I figured it, my biggest problem right now

was the bright green evidence residing in my closet, evidence that was growing noisier with each life-restoring meal. To give myself a break from Jack's impromptu jungle screams, I retreated to the house next door, inviting K to accompany me on a stroll through the neighborhood park.

"It's been a while since you've had time to talk," K was saying. "Seems like you've always got something else to do. My mother and I were starting to worry."

Springtime surrounded us. My tall, comely, girlish companion gently kicked at the tiny white petals in our path, releasing their rich perfume, an annual gift from nature delivered by the breeze that passes through the fragile branches of the flowering fruit trees.

"I've had a lot on my mind," I admitted.

"Music lessons, right?" K guessed.

"Music lessons?" I repeated. "What do you mean?"

"Come on, Fowler," K pleaded, stepping into the street to pick up a wadded-up dollar bill. "You can tell me. There's no need to be embarrassed."

"I have no idea what you're talking about, K," I said.

Placing her arms akimbo, K stopped and blocked the sidewalk. Sternly, she glared at me, contorting her pretty face into a Ronald McDonald frown.

"Now look here, Fowler," she demanded. "If you want to have your little secrets, that's fine with me.

I understand. But I will not tolerate being lied to — not by someone who claims to be my friend. I saw you with Wallace's oboe case the other day, and I've heard you ever since practicing that ridiculous instrument in your room. So there!"

"I haven't been practicing . . ." I stopped my denial in midsentence. "You heard me?" I asked.

"Of course I did!" she fumed.

"Was it a sort of squawking sound?" I prompted.

"You know it was, Fowler!" K exclaimed angrily, stomping a long leg on the sidewalk like a racehorse at the starting gate. "It sounded exactly like someone who knows nothing about playing an oboe attempting to play an oboe!"

Should I tell her? I wondered.

It wouldn't be right to make K an accomplice now, I figured. Besides, isn't that how most criminals wind up getting caught? By not being able to keep their mouths shut?

"I'm planning to take lessons," I announced, "just as soon as I can find a teacher."

"You are?" she asked, surprised.

"No life can be deemed complete without music," I improvised.

"Oh, Fowler, why didn't you tell me this before?" K cooed, her demeanor changing from annoyed neighbor to adoring fan. "My friend Fowler, the oboe player. That's so sweet. Will you play something for me?"

"If I ever perform anything on the oboe," I said, "you, K, will not only be among the first to hear me, I'll make sure you're seated in the very first row. That's a solemn promise."

K gently placed her hand on my shoulder and gazed into my eyes.

"Oh, Fowler," she gushed, "just when I think I've got you all figured out, you do something like this to amaze me."

Jumpin' Jack Flash

According to Thurgood Bleeth, Ph.D., in his comprehensive tour de force, *Bleeth's Complete Compendium for Boys,* parrots that looked like Jack belonged to one of the several species known as Amazons: medium-size, mostly green exotics once favored by explorers, pirates, and kings for the beauty of their plumage, their superior intelligence, their personality, and their entertaining, comical behavior.

Like dogs, Dr. Bleeth reported, Amazons can be quite affectionate, but unlike man's best friend, Amazons tend to be stubbornly independent animals with definite likes and dislikes, especially when it comes to people. In fact, Dr. Bleeth pointed out, Amazons have been known to carry a personal grudge all the way to the grave, a statement of some significance, he said, since Amazons tend to be hardy birds who frequently outlive their owners.

I glanced up from my reading to the half-plucked exhibit swinging upside down in my closet. Jack had a buckwheat pancake in one claw and an orange wedge in his beak. His face was wet with juice.

He'd *have* to be a hardy bird to survive the treatment he'd received at the negligent hands of Mrs. Picklestain and her death-dealing gang of third-graders, I concluded.

"Way to be, Jack!" I called.

"Hello," he replied.

In his book, in living color, Dr. Bleeth had thoughtfully included a chart presenting the twenty-seven species of Amazon parrots. Carefully, I unfolded it and held it up next to Jack. From the few remaining red feathers on his wings, and the short, sparse red and blue feathers on the top of his head, I concluded that my new houseguest was a green-cheeked Amazon, a variety sometimes called the Mexican red-head.

"Not an especially good talker," Dr. Bleeth had noted under the heading labeled "Remarks," "but a child couldn't ask for a better companion."

"Well," I said to Jack, "this is encouraging news."

I reached over and patted him on the head.

In a flash, Jack clamped his sharp, pointed beak firmly into the fleshy part of my hand. Within seconds, blood was trickling down my arm.

"Dang it, Jack!" I shouted. "Why did you do that?"

Holding my hand under cold running water in the bathroom sink, it occurred to me that — Bleeth's opinions notwithstanding — a parrot is not an easy creature to love. In many ways, it seemed, as I watched my lifeblood dribble down the drain, parrots are like snakes with feathers — ornery, bad-tempered, and definitely not to be trusted.

Hmmm, I thought. *Could this be the reason Mrs. Picklestain "forgot" to put food and water in Jack's cage?*

What previously had been black and white about my noble crime of mercy now seemed ominously gray.

Clouds of Witness

Strangely, there was no outcry at school about the missing parrot.

I'd expected the place to be in an uproar, with everybody bemoaning the shocking condition of Mrs. Picklestain's vandalized classroom, angrily demanding punishment for the person who'd purloined the half-plucked bird. Instead, it was business as usual.

There were no police officers with handcuffs, no assistant principals searching lockers, not even an official announcement over the school intercom. It was as if Jack had simply called in sick for the day.

Nevertheless, something gave me the uneasy feeling that people were wise to me.

In social studies, Mr. String, lecturing endlessly about America's westward expansion, suddenly took notice of my absent-minded window-gazing.

"May we have your attention, Mr. Fowler?" he demanded. "Or are you too busy with your bird watching?"

Bird watching? I thought. *Does he know?*

Later that morning, standing with a group of kids by the water fountain talking about nothing in particular, I was taken aback by a room mother who pointed a camera in our direction.

"Watch the birdie!" she said.

Birdie? I wondered. *Whatever happened to "Say cheese"?*

And speaking of cheese, at lunch, once again they ran out of pizza. I had to settle for tuna surprise. I complained about this to K.

"Too bad, Fowler," she said, not entirely sympathetically, "but it's the early bird that gets the worm."

"Bird?" I replied, squirming in my seat. "I thought we were talking about pizza!"

In the library that afternoon, the pear-shaped, pink-haired, newly victimized Mrs. Picklestain, whom I'd managed to avoid every day for almost six years, dropped a book right in front of me.

"Oh, do be a dear now and pick that up," she instructed.

Uncomfortably, I complied, my unease turning to alarm when I saw that what I was holding in my hand was the story of a famous prison inmate: *The Bird Man of Alcatraz.*

Late that afternoon, en route to PE, I passed Vice President Lloyd in the hallway.

"Hello," he said.

Now, normally, I wouldn't place much significance in such a greeting. After all, lots of people say "Hello" and mean nothing by it but "Hello." But on this occasion, I could swear that the amiable custodian was imitating the distinctive singsong voice of Jack.

"Hello, hello," Vice President Lloyd repeated, after which he winked, unless it was the light reflecting off his glasses.

By now, I was beginning to get the feeling that everybody knew what I had done.

"Hey, Fowler, wait up!" a squeaky little voice called out. "It's not like I can fly, you know."

Fly? I thought, turning around to confront my accuser.

The voice, I discovered, belonged to my self-proclaimed new best friend, the parasitic Wallace, who was struggling to manage a lunchbox, a backpack, a baseball bag, and his oboe case. Instead of his customary geek clothes, Wallace was dressed in the familiar purple jersey of the Superior Limestone Rockets. Printed on the back were the words HOME RUN WALLACE, and beneath this, in big white numerals, was the number seventeen.

Hey! my inner voice cried in dismay. *That was my number!*

"I was hoping to run into you," Wallace said, panting like a lapdog. "I wanted to be the first to give you the good news."

"You've already told me," I said. "Remember? Right after the tryouts. Anyhow, in case I didn't mention it before, congratulations on making the team."

"No, not that," my accidental replacement replied. "I'm talking about your lessons. K mentioned you were looking for an oboe instructor, and since you've been so nice to me, I asked mine to take you. Actually, I begged her. So guess what? She'll let you start tomorrow. But you have to call right away. Here's the number."

"Really, Wallace," I said, staring blankly at the soggy, crumpled paper he'd shoved into my hand, "you don't have to do this."

"Oh, Fowler," he replied, clasping his hands together and displaying a disconcerting, rodentlike smile, "come on, now. After all you've done for me, it's the least I can do!"

Calm down, my inner voice advised me. *Breathe deeply, say nothing. Give yourself time to think.*

"Oh, and did I tell you what happened, Fowler?"

Wallace added with a weird little laugh. "While we were at tryouts the other day, something tried to make a nest in my oboe case. Can you imagine? A nest, lined with bright green feathers! I think it must have been a duck. Isn't that the funniest thing you ever heard? A mallard duck!"

Tales of the Unexpected

The problem with choosing crime as a career is that you quickly reach a point where you can't quit your job. It's not like washing golf balls at the country club or bagging fries at Burger King. Once you've passed enough mileposts on the wayward path, you have to follow it wherever it may lead.

The coverup for my parrot-napping was leading me in some strange directions, indeed. The address I'd received from the woman on the telephone was in an older part of town where the houses come right up to the street. Many had been painted bright colors in a last-ditch effort to inject some cheer into a neighborhood that had seen better days. Some of them had also been converted into shops and businesses. I passed a taxidermist, an African violet store, a Tupperware repair center, a restaurant ironically named The Green Parrot, and a beauty shop whose customers all seemed to have pink hair. Finally, I arrived at the correct address, a turquoise, two-story house with heavy curtains covering the front windows. In one of them was an inconspicuous hand-lettered sign that read MUSIC STUBIO.

Hmmm, I thought. *The oboe teacher's name must be Mrs. Stubio. Perhaps she is Italian.*

Reminding my reluctant self that what I was here to do was absolutely necessary, I swallowed hard, shut my eyes, and rapped my knuckles against the door.

"Who is it?" a woman sang out.

Something in her voice reminded me of someone I knew. But who? An elderly relation, perhaps?

"It's Fowler," I called. "I telephoned you yesterday about starting oboe lessons."

"Oh, yes," she trilled, "Wallace's friend. Just a minute."

Waiting for the music instructor to open the door, my inner voice had plenty of time to question my actions.

Oboe lessons? it asked. *Are you nuts?*

I have to throw the hounds off the scent, I replied.

So long as passersby believed that the squeaks, screeches, screams, and squawks coming from my house were just the ordinary flubs of a first-year oboe student, I figured, they wouldn't connect me with the missing parrot.

My inner voice disagreed.

Oh, what a tangled web we weave, it lamented, *when first we practice to deceive.*

Back off! I retorted.

As if taking up the oboe weren't humiliating enough, now my inner voice was quoting Sir Walter Scott!

From inside the house, the music instructor called out, "Are you still there?"

"Still waiting," I answered.

What was taking her so long? I wondered.

Oh, well, my inner voice pointed out, *at least it's giving us time to think.*

Time to think — another interesting aspect about the criminal mind that never occurred to me back when I was legit. Criminals spend lots and lots of time just thinking about their crime. The whole process of planning it, getting away with it, and replaying each detail of the criminal act is fascinating to the guy who did it. In my opinion, this is why prison rarely straightens criminals out. Instead of using all that jail time to figure out how wrong they've been, the opposite occurs: They come to the conclusion that other people are to blame.

Take my case, for example. If someone hadn't left the feather in the hall, if K hadn't suggested that I set the parrot free, if the front door to the school hadn't suddenly come unlocked, if Mrs. Picklestain hadn't so foolishly stuck the combination to the cage — in fact, if Mrs. Picklestain had taken better care of her parrot in the first place — none of this would have happened.

It's not my fault! I thought. *I'm not the criminal here — I'm the victim!*

I continued to stand on the porch of the music studio.

Where is that woman, anyway? I wondered.

From an upstairs window, a big, orange tabby cat poked its head through the curtains, stared down at me, and yawned, a reflection of my boredom. On the sidewalk, a bent-up old man trailing a gray-faced wiener dog shuffled by without speaking. Clanging its bell slowly, as if it had all the time in the world, a fire truck rumbled down the street.

Maybe something's happened to her, I thought. *I'll give her a couple of more minutes.*

The thought entered my head that not everything that's called a crime is really a crime. Except for murder, terrorism, and a few other obviously horrible things, much of what we consider unacceptable behavior is actually just our inability to understand. If people found themselves in my shoes, for example, seeing what I see, feeling how I feel, faced with the choices that I face, it's possible that they would steal a parrot too! My advice is (1) Don't be so quick to judge; and (2) try to get one that doesn't bite.

Has she forgotten me? I wondered. *This is getting ridiculous!*

Once again, I knocked on the door, this time more insistently.

"Hey!" I shouted. "I have to be home before dark!"

With that, the door opened.

"Sorry for the delay," the woman apologized, "but I was right in the middle of grading papers. Please come in."

I hurried through the doorway into the room.

"That's okay," I muttered.

"Why, where's your instrument?" the instructor inquired. "You can't play music without an instrument."

"I haven't exactly had time . . ." I began.

But as my eyes adjusted to the curtained gloom, I stopped in mid-excuse. Suddenly, I knew where I'd heard that voice before. The startling evidence loomed in front of me like a mountain range rising from the plains. Wallace's oboe instructor — and now mine — was none other than the pear-shaped, pink-haired, third grade teacher and infamous torturer of Amazon parrots, Mrs. Picklestain!

Lesson One

If an oboe lesson without an oboe is this bad, I thought, *what will happen when I have an instrument?*

Mrs. Picklestain must have studied music at dental

school. An hour in her clutches was agony.

First, she insisted that I try to sing the scales so she could find out if I had an "ear for music." I'm guessing from her pained reaction that I don't. Then she tried to teach me how to blow on a double reed, which caused my lips to go numb and my mouth to run completely out of spit. This punishment was followed by finger exercises using a broom handle on which Mrs. Picklestain had drawn circles with a Magic Marker. The idea was to teach me which notes were where on an oboe, but when the ink got on my fingers and I smudged everything I touched, the plan was scrapped.

Mrs. Picklestain then resorted to the lecture method of musical instruction, talking on and on and on about theory, compositions, composers, and how the woodwinds are the most important section of the orchestra, and how, when she was younger, she'd hoped someday to play professionally but had to set aside her dream when thieves broke in and stole the family oboe.

"What?" I said in disbelief. "They stole it?"

"In broad daylight," she replied. "Can you imagine? What kind of person could do such a thing?"

"Hmmm," I replied.

"When musical instruments are no longer safe in their homes," Mrs. Picklestain continued, "all civilization has surrendered."

"Did they ever find the guy?" I asked.

"Not yet," Mrs. Picklestain answered, "but I continue to hold out hope for his capture."

"You do?" I said. "How long ago did this happen?"

"Forty-three years ago," Mrs. Picklestain replied, "but I remember it as though it were yesterday."

"Hmmm," I said again.

From the mantelpiece, Mrs. Picklestain retrieved a black-and-white photograph in a silver frame. In it a skinny girl wearing a long black dress was playing the oboe.

"That was taken the night I received a standing ovation at my father's Elks Lodge. I performed three selections by Bach and one by Heckel, all quite challenging. The next day, my oboe was gone."

"How interesting," I remarked, unable to stop staring at the picture.

"After that," Mrs. Picklestain said, "everything changed."

No kidding! I thought to myself, astounded by the dramatic difference between the young woman in the photo and the old woman in the room.

Why is it, I wondered, *that we start out looking like people but end up resembling fruits and vegetables?*

"For a while," Mrs. Picklestain continued, "I seriously considered pursuing a career in law enforcement, but eventually I decided to become a schoolteacher instead."

"Makes sense," I responded.

"Yes," Mrs. Picklestain replied, "teaching elementary school is much more rewarding than being a police officer. That's because, unlike with adult criminals, children who go wrong are very easy to catch. Their guilt is always written plain as day across their sneaky little faces."

Gulping audibly, I gazed blank-faced past the music instructor into shadows.

"Say," Mrs. Picklestain abruptly announced, "you look familiar. Haven't I seen you somewhere before?"

"I don't think so," I fibbed. "I don't get out much."

Suddenly, for no apparent reason, Mrs. Picklestain laughed. It wasn't a friendly, chortling kind of laugh, such as you'd hope your music teacher to have, but a menacing, witchlike cackle, a sound that much like the oboe's sets off a chain reaction of shivers, even on a warm spring day.

She's on to me! I thought.

"Next time, bring your instrument," Mrs. Picklestain said.

The lesson over, I raced home to my parrot. Jack was perched on the foot of my bed, near the window, looking at something outside. He fluffed out his feathers when he realized I'd entered the room.

"Hello," he said.

"Hello," I responded. "How did you get out?"

A quick glance at the closet door provided the answer. All around the doorknob, the wood was chewed and splintered.

"Holy smokes, Jack!" I cried. "Did you do that?"

Jack opened his beak into a lazy yawn. In his mouth was a toothpick-size fragment.

"Oh, man, Jack!" I moaned. "What's gotten into you?"

Calmly, Jack stretched his wings, rotated his head, and with no apology whatsoever, proceeded to release a freshly minted parrot dropping on my bedspread.

"Hey!" I shouted in alarm.

"Hello," Jack replied.

The First National Bank of K

For people who are serious about living a life of crime, it's probably a good idea to begin by getting a lot of money. No matter how much parents, philosophers, and members of the clergy may suggest otherwise, sooner or later, the only way to fix things that go haywire is with cold, hard cash.

Jack needed a cage, not a closet, and the one he'd left behind was not an option. It was too big and heavy for me to carry, and even if it weren't, it was much too risky for me to return to Mrs. Picklestain's classroom any time soon. According to the infallible Dr. Bleeth, the purchaser of a well-constructed cage designed for a middle-size parrot can expect to part with hundreds of dollars. In order to divert suspicion, I also required an oboe. A new one, Bleeth reported, can easily set a person back a thousand or more. Used ones are less but often require costly repairs. Renting one is cheaper in the beginning, he pointed out, but more expensive as time goes by. Then there's the cost of oboe lessons. Mrs. Picklestain was insisting on partial payment in advance.

"It assures me that my students will show up every week," she'd explained. "Plus it includes the annual recital fee."

Annual recital? I thought. *She's expecting me to take oboe lessons for an entire year? Not a chance!*

Of course, I couldn't let Mrs. Picklestain know my true feelings, so I just nodded my head and said, "Okay, sure, whatever."

I considered my financial situation. My cash on hand was enough either to rent a video or purchase a small canister of parrot food, but not both. My trading card collection had plummeted in value once everybody had figured out there was no limit to how many cards the trading card company was willing to print. My baseball trophies had only sentimental value. I owned an electric rock tumbler, but it was busted — just like me. There was a distinct possibility that my great-aunt would send me a check for my birthday, but that special occasion was nearly three months away. I needed the money now.

I was left with two choices: I could disregard every law but the law of the jungle and steal the money I needed, or I could do what so many people do and simply borrow it, knowing there's precious little chance it'll ever get paid back. Either way, I figured, the result would be pretty much the same.

Since robbing banks was out of my league, I turned my attention to the only other cash depository I knew about: the impressive pile hoarded by my friend, classmate, and consistently lucky neighbor, K.

"Five hundred dollars is a lot," she said. "It's practically my entire life savings. I've worked hard for that money."

"No offense, K," I replied, "but you didn't work for that money at all. You found it, every penny of it, and some of it at my house, I might add."

"Finding things is work too, Fowler," she reprimanded. "If you don't believe me, you ought to try it sometime."

I recalled the effort that I'd put into finding the combination to the lock on Mrs. Picklestain's parrot cage. Perhaps K was right.

With the sound of wind chimes wafted by a spring breeze, a solitary timepiece sounded out the hour, while throughout the many rooms of K's mother's house other clocks counted off the seconds, tick by soft, soothing tick.

"Have you ever tried to get all of them to chime together?" I asked. "You know, so they all tell the same time?"

"I've thought about it," K said, "but I can't see that it makes that much difference. If you have enough clocks, it all averages out anyway."

I looked at the collection displayed on every surface in the room.

"You have enough," I observed.

K simply nodded her head. From her silence, I concluded that my request for emergency funds had been dismissed. I put my brain to work on resurrecting the subject. Understandably, this took a while, time that was filled with clock clicks, ticks, and overlapping tapping, a sound like that of drummers forever missing the beat.

"You know, K," I said at last, "money that stays locked away is like a clock that never knows what time it is."

K gave me a puzzled look.

Undaunted, I continued. "That money has missed the chance to do what it was so carefully created for," I said. "It's a waste, that's what it is. An unfulfilled destiny. Like a life simply thrown away."

"Hmmm," K said, cupping her chin with her thumb and forefinger.

"On the other hand," I went on, "money released from its cage and turned loose in the world can spread its wings and soar, joining up with other money to make even more money. It's a lot like birds — free to mingle, loot begets loot. In fact, that's why they call a fat stash such as yours a nest egg."

"I thought you said it was like clocks," K muttered.

"That too," I replied. "Money is like birds and clocks — a little of each."

"Hmmm," K said.

I concluded that by not saying "No," K was on her way to saying "Yes."

My life of crime was about to move up a notch.

Robbery, I began to understand, can take many forms. There's the sneaky kind, in which a thief breaks in and steals when no one is around. There's the confrontation, in which a robber wields a weapon to force his victim to hand over the valuables. And then there's the con job, as much a criminal act as the other two but with the potential for making the victim feel pleased to have been selected. According to Bleeth, this is the method preferred by businesspeople.

It was also the method that was about to work for me.

"So if I give you my money," K said, "you'll promise to give it back with more money added to it, is that right?"

"That's the essence of it," I replied. "Of course, there are a few minor details that I needn't mention now."

"What are your qualifications?" K asked.

"I beg your pardon?" I said.

"How do I know that you'll do what you say?" she clarified.

"K, K, K, K, K," I said, shaking my head as if I'd been insulted. "Look at me. Have I ever let you down?"

At that moment, as K was responding to my invitation to look me over, I found myself sizing her up too. For some reason — a reason that I'll never understand — while K vacillated on the verge of falling for my blarney and surrendering her personal fortune, I was suddenly captivated by her brown eyes, her pursed lips, her countless freckles, and her exceptionally long legs.

My, what a pretty girl! I thought.

"All right," K agreed, pushing the money-filled water bottle on its side and dropping cross-legged to the floor beside it. "Let's count it. But you've got to sign a paper, understand?"

"I just happen to have a pen with me," I replied.

Fowler's Day Off

Who says crime doesn't pay?

All of a sudden, I was in Fat City, living the Life of Riley on Easy Street. I had a parrot of my very own, five hundred dollars in my pocket — actually, since most of it was in coins, it was in *all* of my pockets and a plastic Ziploc bag stuffed into my pants — and in celebration of my successful new career, I had given myself the day off, claiming to be "coming down with something," advising K's mother that I planned to sleep till noon. Meanwhile, while all the other kids were in school, I was going shopping.

Jack was housed in a steel garbage can, which I'd drilled top to bottom with holes. I couldn't see him very well, but I could hear him just fine. If anything, the echo inside the can made the parrot's shrill squawks even louder.

"Sorry, Jack," I called. "But it's only for a little while. When I get back, I'll have a brand-new home for you."

"*AAAWK!*" he said. "Hello!"

"Later," I replied.

Outside, the weather was perfect. A hard rain the night before had washed the planet clean. The air was pure. The earth glowed. The lawns and gardens sparkled lush and green. For a brief moment, my heart went out to those unfortunates forced to spend such a splendid day in office buildings, classrooms, and other cages.

At the music store, I was surprised to see so many people who looked as if they too were cutting school. Some sifted through sheet music. Others examined strobe lights, tested saxophones, or tapped tentatively on drums. A few, wearing headphones, simply loitered in the aisles.

Who are these people, I wondered, *with their strange hair and colorful clothing? What power has brought them here? Is there something about music that I should know?*

Apparently the clerk thought so, because before he would rent it to me he insisted on explaining what a special instrument the oboe is, invented, he claimed, for the coronation of Louis the Fourteenth of France.

"It's been a part of the scene for, like, three hundred and fifty years," he said.

"That's great," I replied, "but I'll only be needing it for a few weeks — just until things settle down at home."

"That's cool," he said.

Without a car to haul your stuff in, shopping gets complicated. I had to walk home to drop off the oboe and refill my pockets with cash before I could buy a cage for Jack. He must have heard me opening the front door, because he hollered the moment I stepped inside. From within his garbage can, he sounded like he was using a speakerphone.

"*AAAWK!*" he called.

"Hang in there, Jack," I said. "I'll be back in a little while."

"Hello," he answered.

I've got to teach Jack some new words, I thought.

At the pet supply superstore it took me a while but eventually I found the well-made cage for medium-size parrots that Dr. Bleeth had recommended. Made of welded steel and painted an attractive jungle green, it had a parrot-proof door latch, stainless steel food cups, and a detachable, portable parrot playground on top. It was just about perfect. The only problem was that it cost five hundred dollars, not four hundred, as Dr. Bleeth's book, published years before, had led me to believe. Even with my pockets bulging with K's cash, now that I'd paid to rent an oboe, I couldn't afford it.

"Dang!" I said.

Discouraged, I walked over to the cages of birds for sale. Trapped behind bars and sheets of glass were tiny finches crowded shoulder to shoulder on a single branch; dozens of blue, green, and yellow parakeets looking listless and bored; a handful of dirty-white cockatiels with sad expressions, limp feathers, and pleading eyes; and in a big silver cage all its own, a solitary eclectus, an earth-green parrot with a yellow bill, bearing a price of one thousand two hundred and fifty dollars.

Holy smokes! I thought. *These things cost a fortune!*

I wondered how much Jack was worth.

Just then, at the end of the aisle, I spied a display

that had been carefully arranged to catch the casual shopper's eye. A handwritten sign explained what it was for:

MANAGER'S SPECIAL. PARROT STARTER CAGES. $99.96.

What the heck is a starter cage? I wondered.

I stepped closer to find out. Cardboard boxes, each about the size of a pizza delivery box, were stacked underneath the cage. Printed on the boxes were the words

VALU-POLLY DELUXE PARROT HABITAT. QUICK ASSEMBLY. EASY TO CARRY. FOLDS FLAT FOR STORAGE.

"Hmmm," I said.

Not surprisingly, the starter cage wasn't nearly as big as the five-hundred-dollar cage, nor did it have a playground or any other special features. Its spaghetti-thin bars didn't appear to be made of steel, and when I opened the door it bounced back on its hinges like it might be a little flimsy, but the compelling fact of the matter was that I could walk out with a genuine parrot cage for less than a hundred bucks!

This will do, I thought. *This will do nicely.*

With tax, the purchase came to one hundred seven dollars and twenty-one cents. Carefully, I counted out four hundred and twenty-nine of K's quarters, stacking the coins on the countertop in front of the clerk. With a heavy sigh, she began dropping them one by one into the cash register, counting softly to herself as she went. When she ran out of room in the quarters' tray she used bins reserved for other coins.

Since this was taking so long, I picked up a copy of *Metropolitan Pet,* one of many magazines displayed at the checkout. Flipping the pages, I came across an article on the care and feeding of Amazon parrots.

Hmmm, I thought. *This could be useful!*

"How much?" I asked.

The clerk, who at that moment had just confirmed quarter number three hundred and twelve, looked up to see what I was talking about, an unfortunate maneuver, for it immediately caused her to forget where she was in the count, which required her to start all over again. By now, however, she'd mixed in my quarters with quarters from other customers, so there was no way she could ever get it right. Realizing this, the clerk scooped up what coins were left, dumped them into the cash drawer, and attempted to slam it shut, only to discover that the cash drawer was too full.

"What was your question?" she asked me, clearly annoyed.

"How much for the magazine?" I repeated.

With one hand I showed her the merchandise; with the other I presented a pile of coins. A dime slipped out and rolled across the floor. With a loud smack, I stomped it with my foot, stopping it cold. Dismayed, the clerk stared at me.

Still trying in vain to force the cash drawer closed, she muttered, "Preferred customer bonus — it's free."

"Thank you," I replied. "Could I have my four cents change?"

After that, I took a break and bought myself a pizza, two cookies, a frozen yogurt, a video game, a rock tumbler, a tennis visor, and a number of other things I've always wanted.

Walking home with my arms loaded, my stomach full, and my pockets running low — with just enough money left for music lessons — I began to understand even more about the criminal mind. This is a mind focused first and foremost on itself. If it has a motto, it's "Me first." Through luck, comparison shopping, and quick decision-making, I'd saved a bundle by choosing an inferior cage for Jack. But instead of returning the difference to K, who'd trusted me to invest it on her behalf, I'd spent it on stuff for me.

Everyone is my victim! I thought gleefully. *No one shall be spared!*

My inner voice, in either agreement or astonishment, raised no objection.

This, I concluded, was the life I was destined to lead.

Fowler Fillmore Young: master criminal!

More Tales of the Unexpected

I had no idea that the world was such a busy place on weekdays.

I guess I'd just assumed that everyone spent their day locked away like kids in school, but the shopping center was busy, restaurants were crowded, and traffic was backed up at every stoplight. Traveling on foot was no slower than driving would have been.

Like a bird overcome by freedom, I whistled a loud and happy tune as I walked down the sidewalk, a parrot cage balanced on my head. A light tap on an automobile horn interrupted my progress. Looking up, I saw the familiar face of Vice President Lloyd at the wheel of a yellow pickup truck. He smiled and waved as he drove by.

Uh-oh, I thought. *I hope he doesn't tell the principal he saw me.*

The successful criminal, I realized, is careful not to be observed breaking the rules. I made a mental note to remember this.

Arriving home, I quickly learned other valuable lessons. One, if something says "Easy Assembly," chances are it means easy for the person who invented it, not for you — especially if you're wearing Band-Aids on your fingers. Which brings me to the second valuable lesson, namely, that if you shut someone up in a garbage can all day, don't be surprised if he bites you when you let him out.

These setbacks notwithstanding, within the hour I'd put the cage together, and, using a handful of sunflower seeds as a bribe, persuaded Jack to go inside. It was a little cramped in there, but Jack must have liked it well enough, because after examining the bars and rattling the door with his beak, he said "Hello" in a very pleasant tone of voice.

Everybody likes surprises, I thought. *Even parrots.*

I then turned my attention to cleaning up my room, with a special emphasis on the disaster that once had been my closet. After half an hour of this, I began to feel sorry for Jack having to be locked up, so I opened his door. Immediately, he climbed onto my shoulder, where, like a pirate's prized companion, he sat quite happily as I worked. Twice I had to change my shirt until I realized I could simply drape a towel over my shoulder to protect against Jack's inevitable accidents.

Jack seemed very happy to be in such close contact. He played with the hair on my head in the same way he preened his feathers. He clucked softly, like a chicken. Nuzzling my earlobe with his beak, he spoke his only word.

"Hello," he said.

"Oh, Jack, can't you learn to say my name?" I asked, scratching the top of his head with my fingertip. "It isn't all that difficult. Just say 'Fowler.'"

Jack nodded his head up and down as if he understood.

"Hello," he said.

"Hello, Jack," I replied in resignation.

That night I went to the baseball game with K.

It was the City League season opener, and my former team, the Superior Limestone Rockets, was up against Nancy's Embroidery Shop Devil Dogs. I'd heard that the Devil Dogs' new pitcher was pretty good.

"Are you sure you're feeling well enough to do this, Fowler?" K asked solicitously.

"I stayed in bed all day," I lied, "so I'm much better now."

By the time we arrived, the Rockets had finished their warmup and were seated in the dugout going over the batting order. Wallace looked like the star player in his professional, all-leather shoes and purple HOME RUN WALLACE jersey.

Noticing me, Wallace jumped up from the bench and waved excitedly, like somebody on the deck of a cruise ship coming into harbor.

"Fowler, Fowler!" he squealed. "Did you come to see me play?"

Sheepishly, I returned Wallace's wave as all the other Rockets stared at me.

"I thought you didn't like that kid," K said.

"I try to be nice to everyone," I replied. "Even the losers."

"How sweet," she purred, grasping my hand and giving it a squeeze.

The game got off to a slow start. The Devil Dogs batted first, eventually scoring one run, mostly on errors. Then the Rockets were up. They played it safe and studied every pitch.

Seated in the stands for the first time in many a game, I found it interesting that every time a ball was thrown, the spectators had something to say about it.

"Good eye, good eye!" the fans cried when the pitch was bad and the batter had sense enough not to swing. "Make him pitch to you!" they called when he went ahead and swung anyway. When the batter just stood there, watching a strike go by, the crowd called out, "Now you know where it is!" A foul tip was sure to elicit the supportive cry "Good cut!" And so it went, with each successive pitch requiring the dutiful repetition of one of half a dozen memorized phrases.

This is like parrot speech, I thought.

Not being a participant in the game, I soon grew bored.

"Listen, would you like something from the snack bar?" I asked K. "It's my treat."

K glared at me. "That's not my money you're using, is it, Fowler?" she asked.

"Of course not, K," I replied. "It's proceeds, that's all."

"In that case," she said, "I'll have a hot dog."

The line at the snack bar was long, and the lone teenager on duty had obviously learned to pace himself. By the time it was my turn, I'd missed the entire first inning and was well on the way to missing the second.

"Dude," the teenager finally said.

"I beg your pardon?" I replied.

"You want something?" he asked.

"Two hot dogs, two large colas," I said, adding, "and make it snappy."

"All we have is Pepsi," he said.

"That'll do," I mumbled, rolling my eyes.

While he was filling paper cups with ice, I noticed an open carton on the counter, just inside the window. In it was bubble gum — not the kind that comes with each piece individually wrapped, but bubble gum that's been shredded and packed into foil envelopes to resemble the chewing tobacco big-league baseball players use.

Now, that's interesting, I thought. *Fake tobacco for kids.*

The teenager who'd taken my order was now slathering mustard onto the hot dogs. He hummed to himself as he worked. His back was turned.

Suddenly, something came over me. For some mysterious reason, I heard opportunity knocking, yet my conscience — for the moment anyway — had conveniently gone stone deaf. It was as if my inner voice were overwhelmed by its evil twin.

No one is looking, it said. *Take it!*

In the years leading to my encounter with Jack, it

never would have occurred to me to steal. Right was right, and wrong was wrong, and I always clearly knew the difference. Certainly, I wouldn't have been tempted to take something I didn't need, something so trivial, so useless as a package of gum. But all of a sudden, there it was, just lying there beckoning to me. I could have it in my pocket in a heartbeat! Unlike stealing a parrot, or conspiring to pin its theft on Wallace, or tricking K out of her money, or faking an illness to get out of school, this one would be a snap!

How can I explain it? I was no longer myself.

The boy who stood waiting for hot dogs at the snack bar window that night was a changed man, so to speak, a boy who'd committed a criminal act and gotten away it, who'd followed up one crime with another, and another one after that — a boy who had embarked on a life of crime. I was not the Fowler that I'd started out to be. I was a criminal on a spree.

With the dexterity of a shortstop reaching for a ball before the spectators can even hear the crack of the bat, I lunged for an unguarded pack of grape-flavored chew, wrapped my fingers around it, and snatched it from the carton, only to freeze in mid-motion with the paralyzing abruptness of a heart attack, come to my misplaced senses, and drop the gum onto the counter with a dull, dead thud.

What was happening to me?

"Where've you been?" K asked as I handed her a

hot dog and a drink.

"Long line, short staff," I muttered. "What's the score?"

"The Rockets are ahead eight to one," she said. "Wallace is responsible for half of that. He hit a home run into right field with bases loaded. I didn't even know he played baseball."

"You never know what people are capable of," I said ruefully.

"I'll say," K observed. "It's like what happened in school today with that parrot — you know, the one you were telling me about?"

"Which parrot?" I asked, startled. "When?"

"Oh, that's right," K said, "you weren't there, so you didn't hear the news. Somebody took the parrot from Mrs. What's-Her-Name's class — you know, the one with the feathers?"

"Oh," I said, "*that* parrot."

"That's the one," K said. "Anyway, somebody took it today. Isn't that funny? I mean, I remember you and I discussing that very thing. Why, if it weren't for — but that's silly."

"What?" I asked. "What's silly?"

"Oh, Fowler, it's stupid, really, but at first I thought you might have done it, but of course you couldn't have, because you were home sick."

I coughed uncomfortably.

"I'm still a little weak," I claimed.

"We could leave now, if you'd like," K offered.

"No, that's all right," I said. "How do they know it happened today?"

"Well," K replied, "apparently today was the day they'd planned to give the parrot more food. When they looked inside the cage, it was gone."

"Hmmm," I said.

A loud *BING* announced a hit for the Devil Dogs. The ball soared over the head of the center fielder. The Rockets' seven-run lead faded.

"The principal said whoever did it must have been a professional," K continued, "because the parrot practically disappeared into thin air — no witnesses, no sign of forced entry, no fingerprints, other than those of a couple hundred kids. The principal said it was almost the perfect crime."

"The perfect crime?" I repeated. "Weren't there signs of a struggle — a few feathers on the floor, perhaps?"

"The place was clean as a whistle," K reported. "But the principal says he's sure they'll catch the guy who did it, because while the thief didn't leave a single, solitary clue behind, it turns out that the parrot did."

"What kind of clue?" I asked.

"Well," K explained, as talkative as I've ever seen her, "it seems that just before the bird was taken, it scratched a word into the side of the cage."

"A word?" I whispered. "What word?"

"I forget," K replied, scrunching her eyes and

pursing her lips in an unsuccessful effort to jump-start her memory. "It was something quite specific about the criminal, though. Something that identifies him. I'm sure of that."

Before it sank into my stomach, my heart leapt into my throat. In the same instant, the crowd on the opposite bleachers rose to its feet and cheered as the Devil Dogs' runner, a missile trailing a plume of dust, stole home.

All of a sudden, it was a whole new ball game.

Jack Be Nimble

Claiming a relapse of the illness that had kept me away from school, I told K that I had to go home. This time, I wasn't faking. The latest news had me worried sick.

What if the parrot had pointed the finger at me? I fretted.

Just when it looked as if I'd gotten away with it, with not a peep from anyone about a missing parrot, it turned out that the irresponsible Mrs. Picklestain simply hadn't bothered to look inside her bird's cage!

Really, now! I thought.

You'd think that in a life of crime, the criminal would call the shots, but *nooo* — once a crime's committed, other, unpredictable forces take over.

And what about the mess I'd made of Mrs.

Picklestain's classroom? How could she have missed that?

It made no sense.

Now Jack, whom I was only trying to help, apparently had told everybody who-dunnit. What an ingrate!

While I considered the disagreeable possibility of life in prison, my long-legged, funny-faced news source strolled at my side, holding my hand and humming a pleasant little melody.

K, I thought. *Dear, sweet K. Maybe I shouldn't have taken your money.*

K interrupted her song to pluck a five-dollar bill from the grass.

"Mine," she said.

She may have lost her fortune, I thought, *but she hasn't lost her touch.*

I left her on her doorstep, and, returning home, trudged up the stairs to my room, where I figured I'd give Jack a speech lesson before calling it a night. It's a pain trying to make conversation with someone who can say only "Hello."

Things, however, seldom go according to plan. I know this as well as I know my own name. But for some reason I never recall this vital fact until after I've been taken by surprise again.

"I'm home, Jack," I called, anticipating my parrot's familiar, one-word response.

Instead, I was greeted with silence — empty,

chilling, absolute silence.

Maybe he's asleep, I thought.

I flipped on the light, expecting to see Jack on the perch in his new cage, his feathers fluffed out, his head tucked beneath his wing. What greeted me, however, was not a bright green parrot, but an empty cage with an open door.

Jack was gone!

Oh, no! I thought.

Again and again, I called Jack's name as I searched the room frantically. He wasn't in the closet, nor underneath the bed. He wasn't on the bookshelf, behind the lamp, or beneath the upholstered chair. As I desperately sought the absent Amazon, my inner voice reminded me that it was Jack for whom I'd betrayed my principles, my schoolmates, and my best friend. And now, Jack had flown the coop.

Jack! I thought. *How could you do this to me?*

Eventually, having looked everywhere, I was forced to admit defeat. The hour was late. Jack was not to be found. With a heavy heart and a worried mind, I plodded down the hallway to the bathroom.

Oh, well, my inner voice observed, *at least you won't have to keep taking oboe lessons.*

I flushed the toilet and turned on the faucet to brush my teeth.

Have you ever noticed how the sound of water plays tricks on your ears? Whenever I'm in the shower, for example, I always think I hear the telephone ringing. This time, in the bathroom late at night, with water cascading through two sets of pipes, I could have sworn I heard an orchestra tuning up — first the string section, then the brass, and finally, the celebrated woodwinds. I turned off the tap, but the noise of the inept oboe player continued.

"AAAWK!"

It was coming from the bathtub. Slowly, I parted the shower curtain and peeked inside. Just as it is true that a sour note from an oboe sounds like a parrot's squawk, it's also a fact that a parrot's squawk is indistinguishable from a mishandled oboe. There was Jack, happy as a clam, playing in a puddle of water that had collected beneath the leaky faucet.

"AAAWK!" he said. "Hello!"

"Jack!" I cried. "What are you doing here?"

"Hello," Jack said, flapping his wings and flinging droplets of water all around the room.

Parrots, it turns out, love a daily bath. It helps them take care of their feathers, and to an animal whose body surface is covered with them — or supposed to be — feathers are a lifelong obsession. I learned this from *Metropolitan Pet* magazine, which I read while Jack, settling down for bed, conducted an elaborate feather-fussing ritual: picking, preening, straightening, and tucking each and every feather into place.

His routine complete, Jack offered no objection to being returned to his cage. Since no doubt it was he who'd let himself out, I took the precaution of wiring his door shut with a coat hanger. Then, as the magazine suggested, I covered the cage with a sheet. Within seconds, my parrot was quiet.

Whew! I thought. *I had no idea that a parrot could be so much trouble!*

"Good night, Jack," I said.

Jack let out a sleepy sigh.

I lay on my back and stared into the thick darkness. It had been a long, confusing day, and I can't say I was very happy with the way things were going. More than anything else, I was disappointed with myself.

What have I done? I wondered. *I used to be such an ordinary kid!*

Maybe it was because I was so tired, or because I was home alone, or because I sensed that part of me somehow had become lost forever, but whatever the unknowable reason, that night I cried into my pillow. Finally, drifting into sleep like a bird on the wing, I offered up a half-prayer, half-apology to the higher powers.

"I'm sorry," I whispered. "About K. About Wallace. About Mrs. Picklestain and everyone at school. And I'm especially sorry I almost took that pack of gum."

Spellbound

At my next music lesson, Mrs. Picklestain was all aflutter.

"They snatched it right from under our noses!" she exclaimed, discreetly removing some small particle from her own. "One minute it was enjoying a rich, abundant life in its very own cage and the next minute it was gone. They didn't leave me so much as a feather!"

Mrs. Picklestain's description of the crime didn't ring true, but I had enough sense to keep my opinion to myself.

"I understand the bird may have provided information about his captors," I said nonchalantly, attempting to assemble my oboe. "Something that might identify them."

"Oh, yes," Mrs. Picklestain replied. "Most definitely. That bird is quite gifted. Brilliant, in fact. That's why I was so fond of it, you see. And now I may never see it again."

With a disconcerting sniff, she handed me a book of exercises for first-time students titled *Oh, Boy, an Oboe!* Turning to the first page, I puffed up my cheeks and blew.

AAAWK!

The pink-haired music instructor grimaced.

"This must be very hard on you," I said, referring to her recent loss.

"You can't imagine," she replied.

"So what exactly *did* the bird say about the people who nabbed him?" I asked.

Again, I blew into the mouthpiece. This time, instead of squawking, it squealed like a piglet.

Man, I thought. *How many animals can this thing do?*

"He said it was someone on a bowling league," Mrs. Picklestain replied. "Either that, or it was a man wearing a derby hat. The principal can't be sure which it is, so he's checking out both leads thoroughly. I'm sure it's only a matter of time before the culprit is safely behind bars."

I put the oboe down.

"Excuse me?" I said. "That's it? That's the parrot's clue? A derby-wearing member of a bowling team? What kind of clue is that? I thought Jack — I mean, the parrot — had written down a name or something."

Sighing, Mrs. Picklestain took the oboe from me and began to reassemble it properly.

"What the parrot wrote was a single word," Mrs. Picklestain explained. "Using its beak to scratch out letters on the side of the cage, it spelled *Bowler.* B-O-W-L-E-R. The principal believes the parrot was attempting to describe the thief's unusual wardrobe — either a brightly colored bowling shirt or a round, black derby hat, sometimes called a bowler. Unfortunately, despite his extraordinary intellectual capabilities, the bird didn't know that *bowler* has more than one meaning."

But fortunately for me, I thought, *he also doesn't know how to spell!*

My capacity for astonishment was reaching its limit.

Obviously — at least to me — Jack had intended to write not *bowler,* but *Fowler!* Just as when he'd written HALP for *help,* the clever parrot was a single letter off! But what can you expect from a self-taught bird raised in a third grade classroom run by the careless Mrs. Picklestain, a woman who's satisfied to spell *milk* MILT and *music studio* MUSIC STUBIO?

But if I can figure this out, I realized, *others can too!*

"There don't seem to be as many people joining bowling leagues as there used to be," Mrs. Picklestain continued. "Perhaps everyone's too busy with their music these days."

"That's one possibility," I remarked.

"And it's been years since I've seen anyone wearing a derby hat," she said. "So whoever committed this horrid crime is going to stick out like a sore nose."

Mrs. Picklestain returned the assembled oboe to me. I pursed my lips and blew across the reed.

AAAWK!

"How much time do you spend practicing?" she asked.

"I don't exactly keep track," I answered.

"Well," she said sternly, "you'd better practice at least three hours a day if you don't want to embarrass yourself in next week's recital."

"I beg your pardon?" I said. "I thought the recital was next *year*, not next *week*."

"Nonsense," Mrs. Picklestain replied. "My students perform at the same time every year. That's why it's called an annual recital. It's always the night before the last day of school."

"Oh," I said, grimacing, "I see."

"Did you bring your payment?" Mrs. Picklestain inquired.

I handed the music teacher a plastic storage bag containing the last of K's money — eighty-five dollars in nickels, dimes, and quarters. She frowned but accepted the bulging package.

"I'll get you a receipt," she said.

The pear-shaped woman sauntered over to a table and began pecking with two fingers at an old-fashioned upright typewriter.

"Here you go," she said, presenting me with a sheet of pink paper. "Now don't forget, three hours every day. I know you got off to a late start, but with enough practice, you just might surprise yourself."

Oh, somebody's going to be surprised, I thought, *but it won't be me!*

Clutching my oboe case and newly purchased music book, I stepped off Mrs. Picklestain's front porch and paused to glance at the paper she'd given me. Typed above the shaky signature of Lorna Picklestain were my name, the date, the amount received, and the phrase "For lessons, recital, and beginner crook."

Beginner crook? I thought. *Surely she meant to say book!*

Didn't she?

A Secret Revealed

Life was much less complicated before I turned to crime. For one thing, I didn't have so much on my mind. Mrs. Picklestain's recital. Jack's housing. K's money. My uncertain future.

Suddenly, it seemed, the authorities were beginning to close in on me.

As if to make it crystal clear that I was not in control of things, when I got home Jack was on the loose again, perched on top of his cage. This time, instead of jimmying the door, he'd removed a feeding cup and squeezed through the hole behind it. He seemed quite excited to see me.

"*AAAWK, AAAWK, AAAWK!*" he said.

"Oh, Jack," I replied. "What am I going to do with you?"

The bright green immigrant from the disappearing forests tiptoed to the edge of his cage and stretched out his claw.

"AAAWK!" he said again.

"What?" I asked. "You want me to come over there?"

"AAAWK!" he replied. "Hello."

Jack hopped onto my shoulder and nuzzled my ear.

"Oh, you want to play the pirate game, do you?" I said. "All right."

If sitting on my shoulder while I worked around the house was what Jack wanted to do, I saw no reason not to let him. At least he wasn't biting me. Quite the opposite. He seemed as happy as I'd ever seen him.

I wondered if Bleeth could shed some light on this.

I removed the well-worn *Bleeth's Complete Compendium for Boys* from the shelf. Under the general heading "Parrots" I found a sidebar titled "Birds of a Feather."

"In the wild," Dr. Bleeth had written, "parrots congregate in flocks, with individual birds often numbering in the hundreds. So impressive are these noisy gatherings that some observers have called them 'nature's most colorful sight.' This memorable image illustrates how intensely social parrots are. Indeed, their craving for companionship is powerful and unrelenting. Thus, to sentence such gregarious and long-lived creatures to a lifetime of caged isolation is nothing short of torture. Without a friend to talk to, a parrot is not a parrot at all."

The doorbell interrupted my research. I ran down

the stairs, and just as I reached the door, the bell rang again.

"AAAWK!"

The screech in my ear was like a power saw cutting into a metal rod.

Jack! I realized.

I'd forgotten my parrot was on my shoulder!

Instantly, I wheeled around and dashed back up the stairs, Jack's point-blank squawk reverberating in my head. If the doorbell rang any more, my senses were too disabled to detect it.

"AAAWK!" Jack cried as I stuffed him into his cage.

"Pipe down, Jack!" I ordered.

I wired the cage door shut, then for good measure, twisted another coat hanger behind the food cup, should Jack be wily enough to attempt that escape route again.

"AAAWK!" Jack said. "Hello."

"Hush, already!" I commanded.

BOOM, BOOM.

Someone was banging on the door.

"Coming!" I called.

In an effort to catch my breath, I slowed my pace in the middle of the stairs. This, it turned out, was yet another in a continuing series of Fowler-size mistakes. The body, it seems, once it's been propelled downhill, acquires a momentum all its own and can't immediately respond to the brain's sudden whims. This is some sort of established scientific principle, but I can't remember what it's called. Anyway, to its credit, one foot did attempt to obey, but the other ignored my instruction. The result was that I flipped forward like a circus acrobat and tumbled end over end to the bottom of the stairs, where I landed with a thud against the door.

"*OOOF!*" I said.

"Fowler?" called a familiar voice from the porch outside. "Is that you?"

My wristwatch smashed, my body bruised, my head shaken and dazed, I picked myself up, only to be struck in the eye by the doorknob.

"*OWWW!*" I cried.

"Fowler, what in the world is going on in there?" K demanded.

Blinking back galaxies of swirling stars, I pulled open the front door and forced a smile for my persistent neighbor.

"Hello, K," I said weakly. "What brings you here?"

"My feet, Fowler," K replied. "What took you so long?"

"Long, K?" I said. "Why, whatever do you mean?"

"I've been out here forever, Fowler," she complained. "I knew you were home because I could hear you practicing."

"Practicing?" I repeated.

"Your oboe, Fowler," K said, exasperated. "May I come in?"

"Why, certainly, K," I answered. "I was just finishing up. I practice three hours a day, you know."

"That's impossible," K replied. "Nobody can play an oboe for three hours straight. Their lips would fall off."

"Well," I said, "I never claimed it was easy."

"Obviously, it isn't, Fowler," K said, "based on the noise that I heard coming from this house a few minutes ago."

"Was there something you wanted?" I asked.

"I wanted to see *you*," she answered, "and to find out how my money's doing." Suddenly, a jack-o'-lantern frown formed on K's freckled face. "Were you standing under a tree today, Fowler?" she asked.

"What?" I said, confused. "Why do you ask?"

"I'm not criticizing, you understand, " K continued. "I'm simply curious. Why do you have bird poop all over your shirt?"

I twisted my head around to see what K was talking about. Jack was no longer on my shoulder, but he'd left an unmistakable calling card.

"Oh," I muttered. "Well, uh, it's, uh . . ."

"Take your time," K said. "I'll be in your kitchen fixing myself a snack."

With K temporarily occupied, I went to my room to change my shirt, hoping to change my luck as well.

Instead, the situation worsened. To my alarm, my lock-picking parrot wasn't in his cage.

"Dang it, Jack!" I called out in a stage whisper. "Where are you this time?"

I searched the usual places in my room, looked up and down the hall, and checked behind the shower curtain. Once again, the parrot had given me the slip.

Rats! I thought. *I've got to get K out of here!*

"I thought you were going to change your shirt, Fowler," K said as I entered the kitchen.

My pretty, brown-eyed neighbor was sitting at the kitchen table with a can of cola and a wrinkled cellophane bag in front of her.

"Listen, K," I said. "I have a problem."

"You're telling me," she muttered, pushing the bag in my direction. "Here, I've saved you some peanuts."

"Those are Jack's," I blurted out.

"Whose?" K asked.

"I mean, I thought those were Cracker Jacks," I corrected myself, "but I see they're just regular peanuts. I prefer something sweeter."

"More for me, then," K replied, cracking open a peanut and popping a salty nutmeat into her exceptionally wide mouth. "Ummm," she said. "One of nature's most perfect foods."

Suddenly, from the kitchen doorway sounded an ear-splitting alarm.

"*AAAWK!*" Jack screeched, waddling like a

football player across the kitchen floor. *"AAAWK, AAAWK!"*

Startled, K dropped a peanut onto the floor. Jack immediately staggered over to claim it.

"Hello," he said.

"Fowler," K sputtered, "I think I'm beginning to understand the problem on your shoulder, but can you please explain why you keep a half-plucked parrot in your kitchen?"

Accessory After the Fact

Confession, they say, is good for the soul, but how much does your soul get out of it when all you admit to is what you've just been caught at?

My confession to K came spewing out of me like soda pop from a newly shaken can.

"I did it!" I cried. "It was me! I'm the guy they're looking for!"

"Calm down, Fowler," K advised. "You'll upset the parrot."

Over the next three-quarters of an hour, I told that girl everything — everything, that is, except what I'd done with her money. I explained how she'd given me the idea for the rescue; how I'd plotted to shift the blame to Wallace, and failed; how the school building was locked up tight, then suddenly wasn't; how I'd raced home with the bird hidden in an empty

Kleenex box, only to miss the tryouts for the baseball team that I'd been a member of for years; how I now found myself taking oboe lessons, facing certain humiliation in a public recital; how my luck was beginning to run out; and how, despite everything, Jack was doing better in my care.

"I know it's hard to believe," I said, "but honestly, he looks so much better than he did. He's much livelier, and some of his feathers are starting to grow back."

Throughout my confession, K listened without interrupting. Finally, when I was finished, she took a sip of her drink and spoke.

"Fowler," she said, "sometimes, when I hear you talk, I think you must be mature beyond your years. But then, when I consider how you behave, I'm amazed they ever let you into sixth grade."

She stood up. Without bending her long, storklike legs, K leaned over and extended a finger to Jack.

"Careful," I warned her. "He bites."

But instead of defending himself, Jack hopped eagerly onto K's hand.

"Pretty bird," K said sweetly. "Pretty bird."

This was a generous remark, given Jack's balding, bedraggled condition, but like all expressions of flattery, it worked. Jack tilted back his red-capped head and cooed like a pigeon.

"I think he likes me," K said, stroking the parrot's throat with her fingertips.

That makes two of us, my inner voice whispered.

"Have you considered just taking him back?" K asked. "I mean, if you sneak him into Mrs. Picklestain's classroom when no one's looking, your troubles would be over."

"Mine would," I admitted, "but his wouldn't. Jack nearly died back there. I can't let them get their hands on him now."

"I see," K said, nodding as she rubbed Jack's bright green cheeks. "Well, then, what about the oboe lessons?" she asked. "Now that I'm in on your little secret, why bother with them? Why not just quit? Then you wouldn't have to show up for the recital."

"I wish it were that easy," I said, "but Mrs. Picklestain already suspects me. How would it look if I dropped out right when her parrot disappears?"

K nodded again. Jack swung upside down from her index finger.

"Hello, hello, hello," he sang happily.

"What else can he say?" K asked.

"Nothing," I replied. "That's the only word he knows. He uses it for everything."

K lifted Jack to her face and kissed him on the beak. He fluffed out his feathers and sighed.

"Well, at least you got a parrot for your trouble," K observed. She smiled at Jack and repeated her endearment. "Pretty bird."

"Hello," Jack acknowledged.

"You know what I think?" K said. "I think the

reason the parrot doesn't talk much is because nobody talks to the parrot. Have you ever tried reading to him?"

"To tell the truth," I explained, "I've been kind of busy lately."

K frowned. "I'll bet that's the story of his life," she said. "What have you got to read around here that might appeal to parrots?"

I scratched my head. "Books for parrots?" I said. "That's a tough one. Maybe Bleeth has some ideas."

"Who?" K inquired.

"Thurgood Bleeth, Ph.D. He knows everything," I explained, heading out the door. "Wait here a minute. I'll show you."

In some mysterious avian rite or inborn form of play, Jack and K were bobbing their heads up and down at each other like mirror images.

"No need to hurry," K called. "I've got plenty to keep me occupied."

I returned dressed in a clean T-shirt and carrying *Bleeth's Complete Compendium for Boys*.

"Here you go," I said, presenting the hefty reference book that had served me so well over the years.

As Jack proudly climbed onto her shoulder, K held the thick volume at arm's length and frowned.

"Why does this say 'For Boys'?" she asked. "Are there secrets in here? Things girls aren't supposed to know? Is there a conspiracy among boys to keep girls completely in the dark?"

I thought for a moment. A sudden pain shot through my eye.

"Well," I hedged, "it's not like we hold meetings or anything."

In a section titled "The English Language," K and I found a paragraph that we thought might apply to Jack.

"Small children and newcomers to America's shores," Dr. Bleeth had written, "will find English less daunting when presented with the work of the language's finest poets. A well-crafted, rhythmic phrase, rich in imagery and rhyme, is easier to remember than plodding prose, and once it has been committed to memory, the speaker forever after possesses something worthy of repeating."

"This guy's not very easy to understand, but I think I get it," K said. "Teach people English by reciting poetry to them. I suppose it makes sense."

"Of course it does," I insisted. "This is Bleeth!"

In a single, synchronized motion, Jack and K cocked their heads at me and stared.

I let the awkward moment pass.

"So, that's settled!" I announced, clapping my hands together, making a sound that caused Jack's yellow, reptilian eyes to narrow involuntarily.

"Maybe you should pick something out," K suggested. "Where do you keep your best poetry?"

"Uh," I said, "my *best* poetry?"

"The really good stuff," K said. "Your mentor here says it has to be *fine* poetry."

"Actually, K," I confessed, "I don't have any poetry books at all. I always found that stuff kind of boring, you know? Nothing ever happens in it."

"Nothing's *supposed* to happen," K explained. "That's what makes it so fine."

She pressed her finger to Jack's breast, lifted him from her shoulder, and held him in front of her face.

"Pretty bird," K said.

"Hello," Jack sang.

"Well, look, Fowler," K said, handing the bird to me, "I've got to be getting on home, but maybe you can just start Jack out with a poem that you learned in school — whatever comes to mind. I'm sure it can't make much difference to a parrot."

K turned to go.

"*AAAWK!*" Jack complained.

"Oh, and one more thing," K added, her hand on the very doorknob that had recently tried to kill me. "Do something about that eye, will you? You look like you've been in a fight."

Sunday, Lazy Sunday

I'll say this for Jack — he's a good listener.

Sunday was the last day before the last week of

school, and I chose to spend it with my parrot. I gave him English lessons for a while, then talked for a long time about my plans, my troubles, and K.

Eventually, however, there was no need to talk. We just puttered around the house together, Jack bouncing happily on my shoulder while I did what chores I could with a bandage over my eye. My doorknob injury wasn't permanent, but my left eye was swollen shut, and the doctor that K's mother took me to advised keeping it covered for a few days.

When you're handicapped, even temporarily, you begin to think about things in a different way. With disability, it seems, comes understanding. As I learned to get around using only one eye, I came to respect Jack for his verbal impairment. Being a bird of few words is not without appeal. In fact, it may well be the key to forming lasting friendships. Let's face it, people talk too much.

Though I could have used some of that long, lazy Sunday to practice for Mrs. Picklestain's recital, stubbornly I never once took the rented oboe out of its case.

I'm no oboe player, I thought. *I'm Fowler!*

Of course, it was all the same to Jack.

One thing that Jack felt strongly about, however, was being locked in his cage. It took me a while to catch on, but apparently my independent parrot saw his hundred-dollar hideout as nothing but a nest. When he was tired, he'd go inside and sleep, but when he wanted to play, or explore, or simply watch the world go by, it didn't matter how inventively I locked him in. Within minutes, that half-feathered, bright-green Houdini would be sitting triumphantly on top. The issue was settled only when out of frustration I gave up and removed the door.

The higher powers, I realized, are on the side of freedom.

I found it ironic that in acting as I'd done to secure Jack's liberty, I'd seriously jeopardized my own. But you can't live your life looking over your shoulder all the time, or jumping at every imagined knock at the door. I had to believe that when all was said and done, I'd get away with it.

K was not going to turn me in — at least, not intentionally. If only I'd trusted her before I took up music! The biggest danger now was somebody figuring out that Jack had meant to scribble *Fowler*, not *Bowler*, on the side of his cage, which I assumed he must have done to get *my* attention, not that of the authorities.

Even for parrots, things rarely go according to plan.

If only I knew of someone who dressed in a bowling shirt and derby hat! But when I pictured such an outfit in my mind's one good eye, the only person who came to mind was Wallace.

Wallace! I thought. *What a strange kid!*

With him, the bowling shirt was a possibility but

the derby hat remained a long shot. For a fleeting moment, I thought about buying those things and planting them on him just as I'd slipped the feathers into his oboe case, but now this seemed like the wrong thing to do.

How did he become my friend? I wondered.

Anyway, I'd already spent all of K's money, a thought that upset me greatly. K was my oldest and dearest friend. I felt terrible about how I'd treated her.

Money is mysterious stuff. It brings people together who wouldn't dare come together for any other reason, and it separates those who never should be apart. Money is more powerful than destiny.

I had to figure out a way to pay K's money back. I couldn't bear the thought of telling her the truth.

After dinner, I took Jack into the shower with me. With a parrot balanced on my arm, I found it tricky to wash myself and keep my bandage dry, but somehow I managed. I could tell that Jack had fun.

I did too.

Shower time was followed by another round of speech lessons for Jack, who listened attentively without comment. When finally I stopped reciting, Jack climbed into his cage and went to sleep. I tried to read my magazine for a while, but with only one good eye, I soon gave up and joined my parrot pal in his dreams. The details escape me now, but those were some of the best flying dreams I've ever had.

Closing In

HAVE YOU SEEN THIS MAN?

The headline screamed from the tile walls in every hallway.

Over the weekend, the displays of student artwork at the elementary school had been replaced with brightly colored, photocopied Wanted posters. Underneath the headline was a drawing of a person in a derby hat wearing a loosely fitting, open shirt with three bowling pins embroidered on the pocket. He looked sort of like the cartoon character Fred Flintstone, I thought, short and stocky with unkempt hair and a goofy grin — a description that in the broadest sense, I supposed, could apply to me.

Hmmm, I thought. *It's a good thing I'm wearing an eye patch today.*

Underneath the picture were the words WANTED IN PARROT-NAPPING. "BOWLER." DESCRIPTION UNKNOWN. THE PARROT, HOWEVER, IS GREEN. FIVE-DOLLAR REWORD.

Reword? I thought. *Surely they mean* reward!

It had to be another of Mrs. Picklestain's typographical errors.

A curious thought flashed across my mind. With a five-dollar reward, I could turn *myself* in and give the money to K as a down payment on what I owed her. My inner voice quickly interjected that such a plan was seriously flawed.

It wasn't the only voice trying to get my attention.

"Hey, Fowler. Weird, huh?" it said.

This time, the voice belonged to Wallace. He was dressed in matching tangerine-colored shirt, shorts, and socks, and, as usual, was carrying his sticker-stuck oboe case.

"What's weird?" I asked, trying not to damage my good eye by staring. An outfit such as Wallace's should be viewed only through smoked glass.

"Somebody stealing Mrs. P's parrot," he replied. "Remember how I found those feathers inside my case? I'm thinking they might have belonged to him."

Perhaps it was because he'd recently taken up athletics, but Wallace had impressive deductive powers. To throw him off the scent, I pretended to misunderstand.

"To whom, Wallace?" I said.

"The parrot, Fowler," Wallace said. "They were green, remember?"

"They?" I asked, shaking my head to feign confusion. "I thought it was just one parrot."

"The feathers, Fowler," he said. "The green feathers."

"Are you sure, Wallace?" I asked. "I thought you told me those feathers were blue."

"No, green!" Wallace insisted. "Don't you remember? It was at the baseball tryouts."

"I don't know, Wallace," I dodged. "That was a long time ago."

A quizzical expression on his face, Wallace stepped forward to give me a closer look.

"Hey, what did you do to yourself?" he asked.

I reached up to the black patch covering my left eye.

"Foul ball," I fibbed. "But I caught it anyway."

"Good for you, Fowler," Wallace said admiringly. "It's not going to keep you out of the recital, is it?"

"Hmmm," I replied, a light bulb flicking on inside my head. "I hadn't thought of that."

At that moment, Vice President Lloyd ambled by, carrying a handful of Wanted posters and a roll of duct tape.

"Morning, boys," he said.

"Morning," we replied in unison.

"Here," the school custodian added, shoving a poster into my hand with a conspiratorial wink. "A little something for your scrapbook."

"What?" I responded with a start.

Why is Vice President Lloyd giving me a Wanted poster? I wondered.

But if an explanation for the custodian's curious action had been forthcoming, it quickly evaporated with the morning bell.

Like a goat prancing in a meadow, Wallace leapt down the hall toward his classroom, and I, much less enthusiastically, plodded on to mine, pausing now and then to reread the Wanted posters along the walls. I couldn't have been more than a couple of

117

minutes late when I took my usual seat, but all eyes turned to me when Mr. String spoke my name.

"What happened to you, Fowler?" he asked. "You look like Long John Silver."

Mr. String was referring to the one-eyed pirate in the famous book *Treasure Island* by Robert Louis Stevenson. I hadn't read it, of course, but I intend to someday when I'm not so busy.

Before I could answer, a gum-chewing wiseacre from the back of the room called out, "Hey Long John, where's your parrot?"

Everybody laughed, just like they do at baseball games when somebody hollers "Foul-er up!"

Things kind of snowballed after that.

Maybe it was the smart aleck who drew them, pleased with the response he got in class, or possibly his quip encouraged those who have no ideas of their own, but before lunch was over, the Fred Flintstone look-alike on Mrs. Picklestain's Wanted posters had acquired a distinctive black patch over his left eye. In some cases the eyepiece had been carefully illustrated with felt-tip marker. In others, it was just a hasty scribble from a passing ballpoint pen. But in poster after poster, there he was, the suspected elementary school parrot-napper, staring stupidly from the walls with his one good eye — a dead ringer for yours truly.

I can tell you, I've had better days.

And the worst, my inner voice suggested, was yet to come.

Coincidence?

"Guilty people invariably call attention to their guilt by acting guilty. The hallmark of the successful criminal is the ability to appear innocent even when caught red-handed."

I was not surprised to find such timely and practical words of wisdom in *Bleeth's Complete Compendium for Boys*, nor did I think it amazing to find the passage marked with a yellow highlighter, although I had to admit that such an occurrence was unusual. But the thing that truly gave me pause was stumbling across boxes of this volume at school. For some reason, I'd thought my copy of Bleeth was the only one still in existence.

How this came about was through another out-of-character move of mine. I may act like a criminal under certain circumstances, but I'm not a snoop. To my way of thinking, other people's business is none of mine.

If the telephone rang and I answered it on one extension while the person it was intended for picked it up on another, I'd hang up within a few minutes. If I found a diary in the street, I'd read only enough to be sure I knew whom to return it to — unless of course it happened to mention my name. And except when a poor, defenseless, half-feathered animal's life is at stake, I don't make a habit of poking around in places where I don't belong.

Curiosity, however, is a powerful force not limited to cats. As I was headed home at the conclusion of that worrisome day, I spied an open book lying on the custodian's chair just inside his closet. Something about it seemed familiar, so naturally I stepped inside to take a look. That's when I discovered not only the aforementioned highlighted sentences, but three unopened cardboard cartons stacked in a corner, each bearing the identical description TWO DOZ. BLEETH'S COMPENDIUM.

Is Vice President Lloyd a fan of Bleeth's? I wondered to myself.

What a coincidence!

But there was more where that came from.

When you're dealing with a planet that's twenty-five thousand miles in circumference, you have to figure that the expression "It's a small world" is something of an exaggeration. But maybe not. Within minutes of discovering the custodian's cache of Bleeth books, something else occurred to astonish me once again.

I had just started walking home, pondering why Vice President Lloyd would need seventy-two — no, make that seventy-*three* copies of the world's greatest reference book — when in the far distance, a bright green object caught my eye. At first I thought it was a child's balloon, since it seemed to be drifting down the sidewalk, lurching from side to side each time the spring breeze gusted. But slowly it dawned on me that it was something that was alive. Soon after, I began to suspect that it was a parrot, walking in that clumsy, staggering way that parrots do. Eventually, as it drew nearer, I could see that not only was it indeed a parrot, a green-cheeked Amazon, in fact, but many of its feathers were missing, just like Jack's. Strangely, it resembled Jack in every other respect too, but I knew that it couldn't be Jack because he was waiting for me at home.

Could this be yet another coincidence? I wondered. *That would make two major coincidences back to back — something of a coincidence in itself.*

Imagine my astonishment when the parrot, waddling over to the edge of the sidewalk to let me pass, tilted up his red-capped head and spoke.

"Hello," he said, in a voice I knew at once.

"Jack!" I screamed. "Where are you going?"

"*AAAWK!*" Jack screeched, flapping his wings.

To this unpleasant noise was added the sudden siren of a police car, which, thankfully, raced past us in hot pursuit of some other criminal.

"Jack," I said, "we better get out of here. It isn't safe for us to be seen together."

I extended my hand. The errant parrot climbed up my forearm and, with much feather-fluffing, settled onto my shoulder.

"Hello," he spoke, nuzzling my ear.

"Jack," I replied as I sprinted for home, "can't you learn to say anything else?"

No Rest for the Wicked

Mrs. Picklestain expressed sympathy for my eye, but not enough to release me from the recital.

"Do you realize," she said, "that many of our finest musicians have been unable to see at all?"

"I think I may have heard that somewhere," I replied politely, "but what I'm wondering is, if they can't see, how do they manage to assemble their instruments? I can't seem to get this one together."

Once again, my music instructor demonstrated how to prepare an oboe for a performance.

"Are you sure you've been practicing?" she asked.

"Not as much as I'd hoped to," I explained. "Other things keep getting in the way."

"Discipline," Mrs. Picklestain replied. "Not only is it the secret to becoming a musician, it's the key to any accomplishment. Now, let me hear you play."

I pursed my lips and blew.

AAAWK!

To my ears, the familiar screech didn't sound so bad this time. In fact, I found myself starting to like it. Perhaps this is an acquired taste, like spicy mustard, hot tea, steamed broccoli, or the company of parrots.

Mrs. Picklestain, however, was having none of it. She shook her pink-haired head and sighed.

"The recital is the day after tomorrow," she said

sternly. "I've already typed the program and taken it to the printer. Your name is listed in that program, Fowler, as are the names of all my students, and just as each of them will perform, so will you — even if all you play is a scale. So my advice is to go home and practice. Practice, practice, practice. There is absolutely no substitute for practice."

"Right," I said, happy to be disassembling the oboe and putting it back into its case. "Practice. Got it." Then, as if I were just making conversation, I added, "By the way, have there been any developments in the case of the missing parrot?"

Mrs. Picklestain wrinkled her already wrinkled face.

"It's interesting that you should inquire," she replied. "Whereas the bird clearly wrote the word *Bowler* just before he disappeared, some of my third grade students are now telling me we should be looking for a pirate. Can you imagine? A pirate operating in these parts!"

"Hmmm," I said, turning my covered left eye away from the piercing gaze of Mrs. Picklestain. "A pirate in a bowling alley wearing a derby hat and carrying a parrot. Why, he couldn't be any easier to find if you knew his name!"

"Yes," Mrs. Picklestain agreed. "The pieces do seem to be coming together, don't they."

A Practice Test

On the day of the recital, K and I were sitting on the floor at K's house playing *The Game of Cheese*. The object of this board game is to own all the cheese factories in town, which you accomplish through skillful play and lucky rolls of the dice.

K was in the lead.

"So you really can't play a single tune?" K was asking me. "Not even 'Mary Had a Little Lamb'?"

"Nothing," I replied. "It takes all the talent the higher powers have given me just to make a loud squawking sound."

"Gosh," she said sympathetically. "And you're still going to go?"

"It's a ruse to maintain my innocence," I explained. "It's what the successful criminal would do."

I rolled the dice and moved my token.

"You owe me five hundred bucks," K said. "Pay up."

"What?" I replied, startled.

I wasn't ready to deal with my debt to K. Not until I had the money — or a satisfactory explanation for why I'd tricked her out of it.

"You landed on my cheese factory," K explained. "The rent is five hundred dollars. Pay me or forfeit the game."

She held out her right hand, palm up, wiggling her fingers insistently.

"Oh," I said, nodding my head. "The rent money."

I counted out five hundred dollars in cheese cash. On a table just above my head, five deep chimes sounded from a china clock.

"Is that the correct time?" I asked. "My watch hasn't worked since I fell down the stairs."

"It might be," K replied, tossing double sixes onto the board, "but I kind of doubt it."

She moved her token twelve spaces to the corner nacho store and stood up, towering over me on her long legs.

"While you're taking your turn," she announced, "I'm going to see if I can find us something to eat. I'll be right back."

"Okay," I replied.

I shook the dice and let them tumble onto the game board, where they turned up a one and a two. I moved my token three spaces to the door of K's provolone factory. With my left eye covered with a patch, I had to squint to make out the rent. Incredibly, it was four thousand dollars! Quickly, I estimated my assets. I had less than eight hundred dollars. The game, it seemed, was over. Unless —

Hmmm, I thought. *K is out of the room. What would the successful criminal do?*

I hardly needed to ask. The successful criminal would throw the dice again, or more likely, not throw the dice at all. He'd simply place his token wherever it needed to be to win the game.

"How does cold pizza sound?" K called.

"Great!" I shouted. "Take your time!"

If I placed my token on the FDA cheddar recall square, which was where a seven would take me, it would force K to close three of her biggest factories. That would certainly tilt the odds in my favor. And if I also helped myself to, say, fifteen hundred dollars in cash, I'd be a cinch to win.

"Do you want pepperoni or sausage?" K called.

"Pepperoni!" I hollered.

On the game board, I turned the first die until it showed a three, then I changed the second one into a four.

The seven easy steps to success, I thought.

As I grabbed the extra fifteen hundred in cheese cash, K called again from the kitchen.

"Do you want a soda pop?" she asked. "All we have is grape."

"I love grape!" I shouted. "It's my favorite flavor!"

Suddenly, from out of the blue, I remembered how I'd so stupidly snatched the grape gum at the baseball game. With the impact of a clenched fist, a terrible feeling struck me in the pit of the stomach.

Ooof! I gasped.

Instantly, my fingers opened to release the ill-gotten wad of cheese cash. I watched as it fluttered to the floor.

What on earth was that? I asked myself.

A message from your conscience, my inner voice replied.

K entered the room with the snacks.

"What did you roll?" she asked.

"What?" I said, recovering.

"The dice," she replied. "What did you get?"

"Oh," I answered, still in a bewildered state. "Well, at first, I thought I might have rolled a seven."

"At first?" K quizzed suspiciously.

"Yes," I said, "but then I realized I'd been approaching this thing all wrong. You see, the question isn't 'What would the successful criminal do?' The question for me to answer is 'What would Fowler do?'"

"What would Fowler do?" K repeated.

"That's right," I said. "'What would Fowler do?' And as it turns out, Fowler wouldn't roll a seven. Fowler would roll a three."

"Oh," K said, confused.

"Congratulations, K," I announced, picking up a can of grape soda and taking a long, delicious swig. "Looks like you've won the game."

From her vantage point overhead, the egret-eyed K surveyed the scene. Unclaimed cheese cash lay scattered near the bank. My game token occupied the FDA cheddar recall square. The dice clearly showed a seven. Adding up the clues, my next-door neighbor sat down beside me, nibbled the pointed end of a congealed slice of pizza, and patted my knee, much as you would pat the head of a well-behaved dog.

"How nice to win so easily," she said. "And now, about that little musical problem you're facing tonight: What would Fowler do?"

On the wall behind K, a clock in the shape of a ship's steering wheel struck six bells.

"I guess Fowler would give it his best shot," I said. "There's only one sound I can make with an oboe, and it's a loud and screechy one, but I'll go out there and make it the best I know how."

"I'm coming with you," K announced, standing to brush pizza crust crumbs from her jeans. "What time does the recital start?"

"Seven," I replied, rising as well. "So I better start getting ready. How do you find out what time it is around here?"

"I just use the clock on the microwave," K said. "It seems to be pretty reliable."

I followed her into the kitchen, where tiny digits on a big steel box displayed disturbing news.

"Holy smokes, K!" I exclaimed. "Mrs. Picklestain's recital started five minutes ago!"

Facing the Music

At one time or another, everyone, it seems, has experienced that legendary dream — or nightmare — in which they're hopelessly unprepared for the circumstances in which they find themselves.

For some, the dream's setting is a final exam in a class they've never attended. Others are alarmed to be onstage, starring in a play, with the curtain rising, having never seen the script. Some report they're in a race car, speeding toward the first hairpin turn. Whatever the situation, the reaction is always the same — panic. At this point, the dreamer typically awakens, bathed in a cold sweat.

In my case, it was a music recital at my school, but unlike the aforementioned examples, mine was no dream. The auditorium, the audience, and the fear that was causing my heart to pound like an entire percussion section were real.

K and I had hoped to find seats in the back of the room so we could slip in unobserved, but apparently that's what everybody at an amateur music recital tries to do. Arriving twenty minutes late guaranteed that the only places left were in the very first row.

We waited for the conclusion of a violin performance of "Oh! Susanna!" Then, with the audience glowering at us in disapproval, we took our seats. I chuckled quietly to myself when I sat down to read the program.

"Look at this, K," I whispered as a third grade girl in a pink prom dress began playing "It's a Small World" on a grand piano not six feet from our faces. "It says MUSIC RECITAP instead of MUSIC RECITAL.

This has to be Mrs. Picklestain's handiwork. She's always making typing mistakes."

"*Shhh!*" K advised. "The pianist can hear you."

As proof that K's observation was correct, the girl in the prom dress loudly struck a sour note. Immediately she stopped playing, turned red, and, flashing a furious scowl at me, started over again from the beginning.

I opened the printed program and scanned the line-up. I saw Wallace listed, and the assistant principal's daughter, and a sixth grade classmate who was always borrowing my homework, and an outfielder from the Superior Limestone Rockets, whom I was surprised to learn played the saxophone (a cool instrument if there ever was one!), but I didn't see my name — not right away. But some surprises happen more slowly than others. Reading on, idly feeding my curiosity, I found what I was not prepared to find located one misspelled name from the bottom of the list.

In the next-to-last position, just above that of some kid named Taylor Schwartz, who'd been tapped to close out the recital with a trumpet solo of "Meet the Flintstones," I saw my name — or most of it, anyway — everything except the first letter. Instead of typing "Fowler," the inept Mrs. Picklestain had listed me as "Bowler."

Bowler! I thought with a shudder.

It was the name Jack had scratched onto the side

of his cage just before he disappeared. Bowler! It was the name on the Wanted posters plastered all over school, the very school in which this recital was taking place! Bowler! A criminal's name, the name on everybody's tongue, the name that fate had accidentally assigned to me!

I was doomed!

"Good grief!" I exclaimed to K, causing the third-grader in the prom dress to miss a chord and burst into tears. "Look what this crazy woman's done to me now!"

"*SHHH!*" the audience hissed.

"What's wrong with you, Fowler?" K whispered. "Is it some sort of death wish? Shut up and wait your turn!"

Frustrated and fearful, I slumped in my seat.

Sharing the bench, a mother and a daughter in matching dresses launched into a dreary classical piano duet that seemed to go on forever. This was followed by a lively little minuet performed by a fifth-grader named Alex, after which, to the audience's delight, Wallace performed a hit song from a Broadway musical, possibly the first time it's been done as an oboe solo. Another kid sang the national anthem, prompting everyone to stand. So it went for the better part of an hour, with occasional whispers, glances, and fingers pointed in my direction each time a performer sat down and the program inched closer to the name of Bowler.

Finally, after a girl named Sarah managed to coax "Comin' 'Round the Mountain" from a patched-up set of drums, it was time for me to go on. By now, of course, everyone in the audience had seen the infamous name, so the murmuring sounded like the buzzing of a thousand bees. Amid this hubbub, one man called out, "It's the bird bandit. Get him!" But for the moment, thankfully, no one was prepared to take his advice.

Mrs. Picklestain had listed Bowler's musical selection as "Various." This was her way of saying she had no idea what I was going to play. In this respect, the typewriter-challenged music instructor and I were on the same wavelength. I didn't know either, but I stood up to take my oboe to the stage, all the same.

"Knock 'em dead, Fowler," K whispered, and for a brief, fantastic moment, I wished I could.

To overcome stage fright, they say it helps if you focus on just one person in the audience, ignoring everybody else, but this, I discovered, was impossible. Everybody from the school was there: the principal, Mr. String, Mrs. Picklestain, the teacher from the classroom next door to Mrs. Picklestain's, Vice President Lloyd, the librarian, the PTO president, all the Superior Limestone Rockets, and a sea of restless kids with curious faces representing grades one through six.

Yikes! I thought.

Once onstage, I sat down on a metal folding chair,

straightened my eye patch, and adjusted the microphone.

The person who earlier had suggested that the crowd "get" me now called out, "It's Long John Bowler! The five bucks is mine!"

"Hush!" said the woman seated beside him. "Let him play his song!"

Calmly, I began to put together the pieces of my oboe. Since assembling it was all I'd learned to do with the complicated instrument, I considered this to be a big part of my performance. The audience, however, expected more, so, casting my fate to the wind, I puffed up my cheeks, closed my eyes, and let the music flow through me.

AAAWK! I screeched.

Immediately, from the back of the room, came an echo: *"AAAWK!"*

AAAWK! I sounded again.

"AAAWK!" went the echo, followed by excited whispers and startled gasps from the audience.

At this unexpected sound, I opened my eyes — or at least the one not completely covered by a thick black patch — and there, waddling toward the stage as rapidly as his nearly useless, twiglike legs could carry him, was Jack! With a frantic beating of his bright green wings, he rose into the air and settled onto my shoulder.

"Hello!" he said.

Several people in the audience applauded, Vice

President Lloyd among them. Encouraged by this response, I let fly with another blast from my rented oboe.

AAAWK!

What happened next is perhaps the most astonishing thing I've ever witnessed in my brief yet astonishment-filled lifetime, and I'm sure that my face betrayed this. Indeed, I felt just like one of those goofy-looking characters in TV cartoons who're always going around shaking their oversize heads, saying "Huh?" as if they can't believe their own saucer-size eyes. But just as this was no dream, this was no cartoon. This was the real thing.

Jack spoke.

With the precise diction of an actor born to the stage, Jack uttered a clear, recognizable English phrase. Opening his long, hooklike beak and extending his nubby tongue until it touched the microphone, Jack said, "A soft-spoken parrot."

Unmistakably, these were his exact words.

Led by an enthusiastic Vice President Lloyd, the audience once again responded with applause. Instinctively, I supplied additional appreciation with my oboe.

AAAWK! I sounded.

Jack fluffed his feathers, tapped the microphone with his tongue, and began again.

"A soft-spoken parrot named Jack," he said.

Amazed at the parrot's unusual, unexpected, and

entertaining performance, the audience vigorously sounded their approval.

Patiently, Jack began again at the beginning.

"A soft-spoken parrot named Jack," he repeated, "longed for the words that he lacked."

This time, the audience held not only its applause but its collective breath, as well. It was apparent that Jack had something he wished to say.

With each new phrase that Jack delivered, I continued to provide musical accompaniment, for by now it dawned on me that my clever parrot, while disregarding the exact words I'd used in his speech lessons, had learned a great deal about the form I chose to put them in. Jack had become a master of the only kind of poem I like, the limerick.

"A soft-spoken parrot named Jack," he recited.

AAAWK! I added.

"Longed for the words that he lacked."

AAAWK! AAAWK!

"But each in due time."

AAAWK!

"Falls victim to rhyme."

AAAWK! AAAWK! AAAWK!

"And now you should hear that Jack yak."

AAAWK! AAAWK! AAAWK! AAAWK! AAAWK!

Amazed, amused, and grateful for this surprising change of pace, the recital audience burst into exuberant applause. The third-graders, being third-graders, stomped their feet and whistled. Vice

President Lloyd rose to his feet and cheered, "Bravo! Bravo!" The principal, not wishing to be upstaged by his custodian, leapt up, clapped his hands, and shouted, "Encore! Encore!" — a sentiment promptly echoed by the entire professional staff.

It was a glorious moment — possibly the finest moment, short of the actual crime itself, that a convicted criminal can ever hope to know.

Bobbing Along with Jack

Whether you're embarking on a life of crime or simply setting out to be an ordinary person living an ordinary life, it's probably a good idea to leave your plans at home. Things never go according to plan anyway. If I've learned anything from this experience, it's this.

Against the tide of circumstance, our meager plans are as futile as a barrier of sand. Far better to be your own lifeboat, and float.

By now, I was going with the flow pretty well. K turned around and hugged me, holding on somewhat longer than mere congratulations would require. Vice President Lloyd, greeting me like a long-lost relative, clapped me on the back and said, "My boy!"

Leading the Superior Limestone Rockets, a beaming Wallace arrived at my side where he proudly stood guard as each of my former teammates shook my hand, followed by the principal, the vice principal, and practically all the teachers. Mingling with the noise of the milling crowd were the melodious tones of Taylor Schwartz's trumpet.

Jack seemed undisturbed by the crush. Perhaps to an animal who's happiest when in a flock, this was paradise. To me, however, it was more than I'd bargained for. I was ready to go home.

"That's my parrot!" Mrs. Picklestain barked, marching up to me. "I've been looking for that thing for days!"

At the unwelcome sound of her voice, Jack shrank his lightly feathered body and ducked his head.

"I'm sorry," I replied, "but I was very concerned about his health."

Clinging with his beak to my shirt collar, hanging down my back like a clip-on ponytail, Jack tried unsuccessfully to hide from his tormentor.

"Well, he does appear to be more active," Mrs. Picklestain admitted. "And his color has improved."

"That's because there's more of it on the bird," I said, "and less of it on the floor."

"And he seems to like you," the music instructor observed.

"I like *him*," I explained.

Clasping and unclasping her hands, Mrs. Picklestain scrunched up her face as if wrestling with a difficult decision. Behind her, well-wishers waiting to shake my hand were becoming restless.

"I'll make you a deal," Mrs. Picklestain announced. "You promise to give up the oboe — no, wait, make that give up *all* woodwinds — and never dare to pick one up again, much less try to play it in public, and I'll give you that bird free and clear. Is that acceptable?"

I reached out and shook the pink-haired woman's hand so hard I could hear her bones rattle.

"It's a deal, Mrs. Picklestain," I agreed. "I give you my word of honor."

"Well, all right then," she said. "Jack, Jack, no trade back."

"*AAAWK!*" said Jack, who'd forgotten he was hanging by his beak. With a disconcerting *CLUMP* he tumbled to the floor. Tenderly, I picked him up and stroked his feathered head.

"Hello," he said.

"That's a fine bird you have there," Vice President Lloyd observed. "Would you consider selling him? I'll give you five hundred dollars."

"Five hundred dollars!" I exclaimed. "For Jack?"

"That's an as-is price," Vice President Lloyd explained. "If he could do sonnets, or even free verse, he'd be worth more, but limericks? That's a very low art form — hardly even poetry at all."

"I don't know," I replied. "I don't think I could part with him for any amount of money. Jack's my friend."

But no sooner had the words been spoken than my

eyes met K's. My pretty, freckle-faced neighbor with the wide, expressive mouth, the girl who'd only recently had her arms around me, was still by my side. When she smiled at me, I heard music playing. It was "Meet the Flintstones."

Five hundred dollars! It was just what I needed to square things with her.

Jack is my friend, I thought, *but so is K.*

"Do you know anything about parrots?" I asked.

Vice President Lloyd smiled. "I was once considered something of an authority," he said.

"On Amazon parrots?" I asked, surprised.

"On everything," the custodian replied.

"I see," I said. But I didn't.

K placed her hand on my arm. "What's going on?" she asked.

"Vice President Lloyd is interested in acquiring Jack," I explained.

The kindly custodian smiled at K. Behind his thick glasses, the corners of his eyes crinkled up like tissue paper.

"I'll take good care of him," he promised. "And, of course, you're welcome to visit whenever you like."

"He'll pay me five hundred dollars," I said. "Which brings me to something I've been meaning to tell you, K."

"Is it about my money?" K asked.

"It is," I confessed.

"You spent it, didn't you Fowler," she stated.

"Not on me," I replied, hanging my head in shame. "Not all of it."

I braced myself for what might be coming next. K could hit me. She could scream at me. Or she could simply take those long legs of hers and walk out of my life forever. Instead, she sighed. Her mouth stretched across her face in a thin, straight line.

"Oh, Fowler," K said softly. "Why do you always make things so hard for yourself?"

I didn't know what to say, so I said nothing.

"And now you're thinking of selling your parrot so you can repay me?" she asked.

I nodded my head.

"I was considering it," I said. "I hadn't arrived at a decision."

Vice President Lloyd spoke up. "Listen, I don't need an answer now. Take your time to think it over, if you like."

"He doesn't need any more time, Mr. Vice President," K said. "The parrot is not for sale."

"What?" I said in astonishment. "You mean, I can keep Jack? You're not mad at me about the money?"

K put her hands on her hips and glared.

"Wrong on both counts, Fowler," she corrected me. "I will not tolerate being lied to. I especially will not tolerate being swindled. So until you give me every penny of my money back, you're not keeping Jack — I am!"

140

"Hello," Jack said.

"Come on, Jack," she said, extending a slender finger. "Hop on. We're going home."

With a long, deep sigh of resignation, I watched as K walked away with my parrot.

"Girls!" I lamented with a sigh. "Just when you think you've got them all figured out, they change."

"The stories I could tell!" agreed Wallace, suggesting a side to him I'd never have suspected. "Why do you think I spend so much time with my oboe?"

Surprise Never-ending

"I guess I was never cut out to be a criminal," I was saying. "The only problem is, I can't seem to figure out what I'm cut out for."

Inside the crowded custodian's closet, Wallace and I were sipping a soda with Vice President Lloyd. The custodian had just surprised us with the admission that he was the one who'd unlocked the front door to the school and cleaned up Mrs. Picklestain's classroom after the parrot-napping.

"It was the least I could do," he'd told us. "Fowler was on the wrong side of the law, but he was there for all the right reasons."

Now, as conversations among like-minded men so often do, the subject had expanded to include philosophy.

"How do I know if what I'm doing with my life is what I'm supposed to do?" I asked.

"Verify the trajectory at its conclusion, not at its commencement," the custodian instructed.

"Huh?" Wallace said.

"Wait until it's over," Vice President Lloyd translated.

His choice of big words where smaller words would do made me laugh.

"You sound like somebody else I know," I remarked. "It must come from reading that book."

I pointed to the copy of *Bleeth's Complete Compendium for Boys* on his desk.

"You've read it?" the custodian asked.

"I consult it regularly," I replied. "Dr. Bleeth is a genius. There's absolutely nothing that he doesn't know."

"Well," the custodian said with a modest chuckle, "although I can't think of anything at the moment, I'm sure there's *something* with which I am unacquainted."

His choice of pronouns took me aback.

"You misunderstand," I said politely. "I was referring to Dr. Bleeth."

"As was I," Vice President Lloyd replied.

From somewhere deep inside me, I sensed astonishment rising, bubbling up like lava thrust from the earth's molten core. I knew this feeling. By this time, firmly into the second decade of my life, I knew it well. It always started out as a nagging bewilderment, a mild sense of confusion, a suspected misunderstanding, followed by a dawning realization that things were not as I had believed them to be, and my plans, however informal, were about to become obsolete.

Tentatively, I sought clarification.

"Just a minute ago," I said to Vice President Lloyd, "when I spoke so admiringly of Dr. Bleeth, you replied by saying 'I,' not 'he.' Is that what you intended to say?"

Behind his thick bifocal glasses, the aging custodian's eyes twinkled. "Although I've gone to some lengths to disguise the fact," he confessed, "the truth is, I *am* he."

"You're Bleeth?" I responded skeptically. "I thought Bleeth was dead."

"Bleeth can't be dead," Vice President Lloyd corrected. "To be dead, you must first be alive. Thurgood Bleeth, Ph.D., is not a person, he is a *nom de plume*."

"A what?" I said.

"Oh, I know that one," Wallace announced. "It means a pen name."

"Correct," the custodian said. "Literally, *nom de plume* means 'a name of the feather.' It comes from an era when writing was performed with quill pens. A *nom de plume* is a pseudonym, a false name, a name that an author uses in order to keep his true identity a secret. Here, let me show you."

Using one of the many keys from his enormous, circular key chain, Vice President Lloyd slit open a carton of books and removed a mint copy of *Bleeth's Complete Compendium for Boys*. Unlike mine and the one on his desk, this one wore a colorful dust jacket. Expertly, he flipped to the inside back cover, where he pointed to a printed panel headlined "About the Author." There, stuck inside a paragraph citing various academic achievements, was a photograph of a much younger version of Vice President Lloyd.

"It's you," Wallace stated.

It was true. Thurgood Bleeth, Ph.D., was none other than my elementary school custodian. You could have knocked me down with a parrot feather!

"But this is a great book!" I exclaimed. "Why wouldn't you want to take credit for it?"

The custodian's face turned red. "I've always hated my name," he explained. "Since I was a boy in school, 'Lloyd Tweedle' has been an albatross around my neck. Kids made fun of it. Teachers giggled when they said it while calling the roll. So the moment I had an opportunity to change it, I did."

I started to say, "You mean, you could have chosen any name in the whole wide world and you chose Thurgood Bleeth?" but my inner voice suggested

144

that I say instead, "It's a memorable name for an unforgettable book."

"Thank you," Vice President Lloyd replied, shaking my hand warmly. "It's always a pleasure to meet a fan."

The next day, to everyone's delight, school let out for the summer — three long months. Coincidentally, my birthday, I realized, was just three months away.

Hmmm, I thought, *instead of a book this time, I wonder if I can get my great-aunt to send me money — say around five hundred dollars. I know she has it. All I've got to do is come up with a plan!*

I opened the door to my house. The smell of halibut frying told me my mother was home.

Limerick for Oboe or *AAAWK*

A soft-spoken parrot named Jack
Longed for the words that he lacked.
But each in due time
Falls victim to rhyme
And now you should hear that Jack yak.

ABOUT THE AUTHOR

Richard W. Jennings was born in Memphis, Tennessee, and educated at Rhodes College, where he won first place in the Southern Literary Festival. The author of *The Tragic Tale of the Dog Who Killed Himself* (Bantam Books, 1980), *Orwell's Luck* (Houghton Mifflin, 2000), *The Great Whale of Kansas* (Houghton Mifflin, 2001), and many essays, articles, and short stories, he is a cofounder of Rainy Day Books, a popular Kansas City area bookstore, and the former editor of *Kansas City Magazine*. He has five children, five grandchildren, a dog, two cats, and a parrot, and lives in Leawood, Kansas.